ONLY A MATTER OF TIME

*

'In the darkness of King Charles's bedroom,
Davie lay awake thinking of clocks and boats,
boats and clocks.
Boards creaked, and further down the corridors
Festival visitors shut distant doors. Then the
house grew silent. Moonlight, shining through
thin curtains faintly illuminating the panelled
walls. And still Davie lay awake, thinking of
clocks and boats.'

Also in Arrow Books by V. C. Clinton-Baddeley

My Foe Outstretch'd Beneath the Tree

V. C. Clinton-Baddeley

Only a Matter of Time

ARROW BOOKS

ARROW BOOKS LTD
3, Fitzroy Square, London W.1

An Imprint of the Hutchinson Publishing Group

London Melbourne Sydney Auckland
Wellington Johannesburg Cape Town
and agencies throughout the world

*

First published by
Victor Gollancz Ltd 1969
Arrow edition 1974

*Made and printed in Great Britain
by Hunt Barnard Printing Ltd,
Aylesbury, Bucks*

ISBN 0 09 908360 4

for
Wallace
9.12.18 – 9.12.68

ONLY A MATTER OF TIME

Friday

I

"ROBERT! BREAKFAST!" MRS. COPPLESTON HAD A SPECIAL
voice for calling upstairs, musical and cheerful, seeming to
promise yet another radiant day for the Coppleston family.
And Robert Coppleston, who had just finished his deep
breathing exercises by the open window, called out "Coming,
Mother!" in exactly the same cheerful voice. There was an
unspoken understanding between them that theirs was a
happy home and that Mrs. Coppleston was the fount and
origin of all its pleasures.

Robert had been four when his father died, and that was
thirty years ago. He could remember the funeral, for there
had been strange men in the house, and flowers, and it had
rained very hard. He could see the umbrellas and his mother
and Aunt Effie and Aunt May getting into a car. But his
father he could not remember. The only influences in his life
had been his mother, and, until they married and went
away, the two aunts. He had no brothers or sisters, no
cousins that he ever saw, and no uncles. From the first he

had been a delicate child—"not the strongest of the strong," as Mrs. Coppleston used to say. But many boys are delicate. It is their business to grow out of it. Mrs. Coppleston had been so anxious to protect her son that she had encircled him. Everyone liked Robert: he had brains, he was good at his job and valued by his employers. But Mrs. Coppleston's love had killed something in him. He had reached the age of thirty-four without ever becoming entangled with a young woman. Many of the girls at the tennis club had set their skirts at Robert, but if he had occasionally taken a mild interest in one of them, Mrs. Coppleston had always perceived something unsuitable in the acquaintance, and had always been able to explain to Robert that he would do better to wait, and since Robert had been brought up to believe in Mrs. Coppleston's well-known gift for the reading of character, he had accepted her judgments, and was glad of her ingenious devices at difficult turnings in his life. "If Mrs. Camperley asks you to tea, say you're engaged," she would tell him. "It is perfectly true. You are engaged to me."

Perhaps Robert had never been very strongly endowed with masculine desire. Certainly he had been brought up by Mrs. Coppleston in such a state of innocence that even now he was not intimately informed about the mysteries of the flesh. Very willingly he devoted his energies to other things. He was a great gardener. At one time he had spent hours with a model railway. In the last few years he had discovered a passion for china. The house was overflowing with Staffordshire figures and Robert had become an authority on the subject.

He did not smoke; he drank very little. He did not drive a car. It was, Mrs. Coppleston supposed, these savings that enabled her son to spend so much on his hobby, but, even so, she often wondered how he was able to make his money go so far. But these thoughts were unspoken. Mrs. Coppleston truly believed that she should not interfere with Robert's life—except, of course, to protect him from dangerous females. For herself, she did not much like the Staffordshire figures. She never admitted this. It was enough that her son liked them—though there was another collection that he loved better, one that existed at present only in imagination, except for one lonely piece of blue and pink and gold, a Meissen Venus with Cupids, that stood on the mantelshelf in his bedroom, opposite the end of the bed. It was the last thing he looked at at night, and the first thing he saw in the morning. You could not compare the Staffordshire figure of Wesley, preaching, with that.

When Mrs. Coppleston called upstairs Robert was standing before his looking glass, sleeking back his hair. "Coming, Mother!" he called back in the appropriate voice. He adjusted his tie, put on his jacket, lingered for a moment in front of the Venus with Cupids, and then quietly let himself out of his room. As he went downstairs he assumed, almost unconsciously, the cheerful manner traditionally expected at his mother's breakfast table.

Mrs. Coppleston, as she considered, had married rather below her social position, and she had spent a lifetime endeavouring to keep, not so much up with the Joneses, as a little way ahead of them. The gay, gracious manner (which had irritated so many people over the years) had been her principal means to this end.

"Tell me about your day, Robert," said Mrs. Coppleston, lifting a purple tea cosy from an octagonal china teapot.

Mrs. Coppleston was strong on cosies. There was another one for the electric toaster. A toaster really belonged to the kitchen, she felt, and so, if it appeared in the dining room, as soon as it had done popping up pieces of scorched bread, its inelegancies were squarely covered in chintz. Mrs. Coppleston liked things to be dainty, and at the same time rather entertaining. Robert hated the toaster cover. But he never said so.

"Busy," Robert answered. "There's a board meeting."

"Dinner at the usual time?"

"Yes; they can't go on talking later than five."

"And tomorrow—the garden, I expect."

Mrs. Coppleston had no talent for gardening, but she liked the front aspect of Morton Lodge to be an example to the other houses in the road. She was hopeful that the lawn would be cut this weekend.

"You're wrong," said Robert. "Tomorrow I'm going to Roughton in the morning, because I want to call at Merry's."

Mrs. Coppleston inwardly sighed. More of those Staffordshire figures.

"And afterwards I'm going to Witherby. The garden's open and it's the best time of the year. Then I'll come back to King's Lacy. It's the first day of the Festival and the opening concert's at Lacy. Of course I'm going."

Mrs. Coppleston did not need to be told that the lawn must wait. Lacy Hall was the home of Sir Philip Gossamer, chairman and patron of the King's Lacy Music Festival, and chairman, too, of Bexminster Electronics Ltd. Robert was the secretary of Bexminster Electronics. Mrs. Coppleston was already thinking that Robert might be seen speaking to Sir Philip. But Robert was thinking that he would have a chance to look at Sir Philip's china.

"You won't be late, Robert? Tomorrow, I mean."

"I don't suppose so. These concerts are over by ten o'clock usually."

"About ten-thirty, then?"

"More like eleven-thirty. I really can't say. I may meet people."

This cross-questioning about his hourly movements always irritated Robert. He had never been a late bird. He played bridge sometimes, and went to the tennis club dances, but, even so, he was seldom out after twelve except during the King's Lacy Festival. King's Lacy was five miles from Bexminster. Of course he wouldn't be back by ten-thirty.

Mrs. Coppleston had made it a practice all her life to make sure that Robert was home before dropping off to sleep herself. When Robert was out her bedroom door was always left ajar and Robert had never succeeded in outwitting her. Taking off his shoes in the hall and tiptoeing upstairs availed him nothing. Nearly always as his hand was on his bedroom door a still cheerful voice would call from across the landing, "Robert! Is that you?" And then he would have to go to his mother's room and say goodnight. Occasionally he had got into bed undetected: but that had only brought a greater retribution, for presently his door would open and his mother would peer into the room. "Robert! Robert! Are you there? I have been so anxious, dear. I did not hear you come in. I wish you would always come to my door."

Robert and his mother never had words about anything, but there were unresolved antagonisms between them which the cheerful manner barely concealed. This was one of them.

"I don't like to think of you bicycling at that time of night," said Mrs. Coppleston.

Robert got up from the table. "I've been doing it for seventeen years, Mother. If I went roaring about on a motor bike you might worry. I must be off."

"Goodbye, dear."

Presently, standing by the window, Mrs. Coppleston

13

watched him wheeling his bicycle from behind the escalonia hedge which neatly concealed the shed from the road. As he reached the garden gate she waved a valedictory hand and Robert waved back. It was an established ritual.

He was only going a mile down the road to Bexminster Electronics.

II

At two o'clock Robert Coppleston opened the board room door. He wanted to make sure that Miss Jesmond had made all the arrangements proper to a board meeting. The long mahogany table shone like a lake in the sunshine. In the center was an island of wallflowers. That was Robert. Miss Jesmond was not sure about the propriety of flowers at a board meeting. Round the edge of the table six places were laid, as for a meal—ashtray, agenda, minutes, pad for note-taking, and a sharpened pencil all round. Miss Jesmond, Robert reflected, must have a formidable store of scarcely-used pencils. They were always new at board meetings.

Robert looked at the table and imagined it furnished with directors. At the head, Sir Philip. Himself on Sir Philip's right. And on Robert's other side, Daniel Caske. On Sir Philip's left, Alec Rowan, Foxy Rowan. Beyond him, Mr. Carroll, and beyond him Joe Major. There was no place set next to Mr. Caske. That was Miss Jesmond's place. She would bring her own impedimenta—shorthand book, pencils, and indispensable handbag.

For a few moments these shades occupied his mind. Robert liked Sir Philip, and he liked William Carroll and Joe Major. Mr. Carroll had a beautiful garden. Robert had been there on days when it was open to the public. Most of these commercial chaps had no thought beyond the new razor blade or whatever it was. But Mr. Carroll knew how to spend his money, and of course he got called a playboy for his trouble. He was not a playboy. He had served in the last two years of the war, and in pretty tough company.

Joe Major was a tweedy teddy bear of a man. Some people said he drank too much. Some people found him a bit heavy, and certainly he thought nothing of saying that he found a report "initially helpful in determining areas related to the study of the problem before us as of now." On the other hand it was rumoured that Joe Major had had thirty years of uninterrupted success with the girls. He must (so Robert conjectured) have been possessed of certain skills not immediately apparent at a board meeting. Besides, there was a naughty look in his eyes. Robert couldn't help liking Joe Major.

He was less amiably disposed towards the other two. He had never liked Daniel Caske from the day when he first announced that he was a self-made man, and proud of it. There's no such thing, Robert used to think; and the man who believed he did it all himself needn't add "and proud of it." That's obvious. There is the famous Sin, raising its head with banners. *He* may forget, but the small people who have helped him on his way remember. Robert remembered. He did not like Mr. Caske.

Alec Rowan was known to everyone in Bexminster Electronics as Foxy Rowan. This was partly because of his appearance, small, sharp-nosed, sandy-haired. And partly because he lived up to his looks. Rowan had a remarkable gift for walking quietly along corridors. Perhaps a managing director, like a sergeant-major, needs to separate himself from the others, the better to rule. Mr. Rowan had certainly achieved separation.

Robert walked to the window and looked down on the

circular drive. Sir Philip's Rolls-Royce was just drawing up to the doorway. In the directors' car park, away to the left, Daniel Caske was getting out of his Bentley. Mr. Carroll's Jaguar was turning in at the gate.

"We're off," thought Robert, and went back to his office to collect files.

"They must decide today," he said to himself.

III

They would have to decide today. As he drove from King's Lacy, Sir Philip, too, had been thinking about the *dramatis personae* at Bexminster Electronics. They would have to decide today—and how did one keep a simple secret in these unfriendly times. People talked about microphones and microdots. They didn't need microphones and microdots if they had a convincing person planted in a strategic position. There was only one defense against that sort of thing, and that was to employ people you could totally trust. What a hope! No doubt the Foreign Office thought it could trust Philby. And where did one look? Did one search the hearts of directors? They made decisions, but who recorded them? And who had access to the records? There were no such things as secrets except the ones locked in your own heart. And so all one could do was to look at people and wonder.

As Sir Philip twisted round the lanes in that still wonderfully empty countryside, familiar faces ranged before him. Joe Major, a bit solemn, but a man of splendidly exact knowledge. Alec Rowan, cold, deeply reserved, but a first-class manager. Daniel Caske—a great show-off but a great man. People said William Carroll was too interested in his own pleasures. What of it? He was a likable chap, and a great source of humour and amiability at a board meeting.

Who else? Mr. Coppleston knew all the secrets. But he surely was totally devoted to the firm. Miss Jesmond? Well, from that point onwards one needed a detective. Who in Bexminster Electronics was in love with whom? Who in Bexminster Electronics had too much money? Who in Bexminster Electronics was mesmerized by foreign propaganda?

Ideas are not confined by frontiers, thought Philip Gossamer, slowing down for the benefit of an ancient sheep dog which had incontinently elected to cross the road as soon as he heard the car coming. Ideas are not confined by frontiers. They flourish in similar climates. Two inventors on opposite sides of the world will come out with the same conclusions within weeks of each other. There are always rival claimants to great discoveries. But the application of great discoveries is another matter. When some mechanical device appears in Japan within weeks of its perfection in England, or when a sales campaign is neatly anticipated by another sales campaign—there is a reason. There had been a reason last October, Sir Philip was thinking, but no one ever found out what it was; or, not to put too fine a point upon it, who it was.

The thought lasted him as far as the front door. Foxy Rowan was waiting for him in the hall. They went upstairs to the board room together.

It was not a long meeting. All they had to decide was the date. Two dates. The first publicity and the follow-up.

"I need not remind the board," said Alec Rowan, "that these dates must be kept absolutely secret."

The other directors looked down their noses. It had to be said—just as a barrister has to tell a jury the ancient news that they must be convinced "beyond all reasonable doubt." It has to be said, but the moment of saying it is always vaguely embarrassing. And so they looked down their noses and examined their note pads.

All of them, except Robert Coppleston, had written down the dates, and had then proceeded to decorate them in their own characteristic manner. Sir Philip had transfigured his into flowers of tropical luxuriance. Foxy Rowan had surrounded his with a number of boxes in diminishing perspective. Joe Major had drawn a pyramid of nearly perfect circles: he had a gift for that sort of thing. Daniel Caske had made an unfortunate drawing of something which might have belonged to a particularly virile Maori chief. William Carroll had made a picture of Daniel Caske and had subsequently folded it into a boat, which now lay reflected on the placid surface of the mahogany lake. All of them had drawn something. But, apart from the dates, none of them had made any notes with Miss Jesmond's beautiful pencils—except Daniel Caske, who, while Joe Major was speaking, had written down a four-letter word in the plural, and then, prudently but imperfectly, scratched it out again.

Miss Jesmond had kept an interested eye on the various artists. After the meeting she was going to take the doodles home to add to her entertaining collection.

"If no one has anything further to say," said Sir Philip, "I declare the meeting closed."

Miss Jesmond handed round tea.

"What's the time?" asked Joe Major.

"You've been asking the time ever since I first knew you," said Daniel Caske. "Why don't you get a watch?"

"Because it would stop. On me they always do. It seems I'm a storehouse of electricity."

"Dear man, of course you are," said William Carroll. "You are Bexminster Electronics incarnate. You suffer for your selfless devotion to the cause."

"I still want to know the time."

"Three thirty-five," said Alec Rowan.

"I suppose you're up to your eyes in this Festival," said Caske to Philip Gossamer.

"Not a bit of it."

"You lend your name and your house and your money—"

"Yes, but I don't *do* anything."

"You've got to *go* to all the things, haven't you?"

"I can face that."

"Rather you than me. What the hell does it cost you?"

"I'm not the only person supporting the Festival. The Arts Council for one—"

"Exactly!" said Caske, suddenly indignant. "The Arts Council! My money! The public's money! Who said I want to support any music festivals?"

Caske had a peculiar genius for getting in a fury in the fewest possible words.

"For the rest of this conversation," said William Carroll sweetly, "may I refer you back to this time last year? Sorry. I must be off."

"Coming tomorrow?"

"Certainly."

"Alec?"

"Not string quartets—not even at Lacy. But I'm going to the opera next week."

"You needn't ask Joe," said Daniel Caske. "He knows about as much about music as a constipated emu."

"Too true," said Joe Major.

Philip Gossamer turned to Robert. It was a moment that Mrs. Coppleston had foreseen in bright imagination.

"What about you, Coppleston?"

"Yes, I'm coming, Sir Philip."

"Good. I'll look out for you."

And "I bet you will," thought Robert Coppleston, collecting files. Still, it was something to have a nice warm flannelly remark addressed to one. Robert was pleased.

"Goodbye, Miss Jesmond."

"Goodbye, Sir Philip."

Miss Jesmond saw the gentlemen to the door, shut it, and returned to the table to tidy up. She couldn't help smiling at Mr. Caske's doodle. It was always the same with him. Mr. Caske was a scream.

Miss Jesmond carefully removed the top sheet from each pad and popped them all in her handbag together with Mr. Carroll's boat (she had a fleet of these at home). Then she gathered the pads and pencils to her bosom and bore them off to the stationery cupboard.

It was not yet four. Miss Jesmond resolved on a long tea break, and peeping into Miss Moone's office on her way to the canteen, she succeeded in luring her to similar indulgence. They had plenty to talk about—in particular the behaviour of the casting committee of the amateur dramatic club.

"Jane Stansley has had a principal part twice running," said Miss Moone.

"And we all know why," said Miss Jesmond.

"It's not as though she were particularly good."

"Exactly," said Miss Jesmond. "In my opinion, you should have had the part, Elsie."

"I'm not saying that, Beryl."

"Well, I am. You'd have been just right as the Queen. Just think how good you were as Marie Antoinette."

It was a very pleasant tea break; but Miss Moone was not shown the treasures in her friend's handbag. That was a pleasure entirely private to Miss Jesmond.

IV

Joe Major lived at King's Lacy, five miles from Bexminster, William Carroll a few miles further on, at Combe Magna. Alec Rowan and Daniel Caske lived over the shop, so to speak.

Alec Rowan's house was in the outskirts of Bexminster, in a road which, according to the modern whimsy, was called Philpot Way, but, unlike the Pilgrims' Way, or the Fosse Way, or the Appian Way, was on the way to nowhere, being bent round in a graceful ellipse, with both ends debouching into the highroad to King's Lacy.

The houses in Philpot Way (Philpot after Councillor George Philpot, a past chairman of the Housing Committee) were detached and well set back from the road. They had neat hedges and neat lawns with room for a weeping willow in one corner, and a double garage at the side. Good things, all of them, but the thing that really attracted the ladies who lived in these desirable residences was that word "Way." It made them feel superior to anyone living in the neighbouring roads. It would be better, of course, to live in the Close, in the shadow of the Abbey, despite the draughty Queen Anne rooms and the Early Victorian plumbing, but, next to the Close, Philpot Way was undoubtedly the best address in Bexminster and nobody lived there who had not collected a pretty good treasure. Alec Rowan had taken a house there to satisfy the pride of Maureen. He could afford it, so why not? But he had small pleasure of it himself.

On this Friday afternoon he left the car in the garage and walked down a brick path with the house on his left and on his right a broad herbaceous border, and the lawn.

And there they were—Maureen's gnomes, sharing an in-

terminable joke across a spotted red toadstool. Alec had re-
fused to call his house "Restabit" or "Journey's End," had
stood out with commendable zeal for the plain number 12 on
the gate. He could not fight over everything. He had admitted the gnomes, but they infuriated him. Every time he
came home he harboured a mad hope that they might have
gone away, or been playing leapfrog—anything rather than
telling the same endless anecdote. But there they were and
they were symbolic of the boredom that reigned on the other
side of the front door. For Maureen was past mistress of the
cliché and was devoting her life (so it seemed to Alec) to
the training of Sonia in the same dismal accomplishment. It
had been rather touching at four years old when Sonia had
said "I've only got two pairs of hands, Daddy," but she was
six now and knew how many hands she had. It was a cruel
bore to be told.

Alec opened the front door. The hall was full of flowers.
The dining room door was open. More flowers, and the table
laid for four. He had forgotten: people were coming in for
bridge.

Alec opened the drawing room door. It was a pretty room
with wide windows on both sides. He strolled across and
looked into the front garden. There was the gnome still telling his story to his two friends by the red spotted toadstool.
He turned to the other side of the room and looked into the
back garden. In the far corner was a swing for Sonia. In the
center of the grass was a lily pond. On the edge a gnome sat
fishing. Alec fell to wondering what was the difference between a gnome and a classical statue set in a perspective of
yew hedges. A classical statue in a grove, he decided, is a
tribute to the genius of the place: it does not pretend to *be*
the genius of the place. It was the gnome's lamentable
pretense at being alive that was so offensive.

Alec turned back into the room and looked about him. He was silly to be so put out by those idiotic gnomes. This was a good room and there were good things in it.

From a long low table by the sofa he picked up a coloured brochure about holidays in the Caribbean. A few years ago it would have seemed a lot of money to Alec Rowan. It was still a lot of money, and he was looking forward to paying it. They would go in January.

A porcelain clock on the center of the mantelshelf pointed its hands to half past four. Supported on the backs of three accommodating dolphins, it was being guided through the waters by two sportive mermaids: and where on sea did they propose to put it, Alec always wondered. It was a splendid piece of nonsense. Coppleston (on the only occasion he had been invited to the house) had said it was valuable, which was as well, considering what Alec had paid for it.

And then the dolphins and the mermaids reminded him that Maureen had taken Sonia to the swimming gala: they would be back by five. He went down the corridor to the study. This was his favourite room, where he read, where he did not have to look at television, where he wrote his letters.

There was a letter to be written now. Well—typed: it was years since Alec had positively written a letter. For him the dictaphone, or, at home, the typewriter, which he played with two fast fingers.

For a few moments he paced thoughtfully up and down the room. Then he sat down at his table and inserted an envelope in the works. He always began with the envelope.

Two minutes later he heard the front door open. Sonia came running down the passage.

"Daddy!"

Alec took her in his arms. "How was it, sweetheart? Did you win a race?"

"Well not exactly I didn't, but I was third, and I got half-a-crown."

"Half-a-crown! Goodness! You have had a day."

"All work and no play makes Jack a dull boy," said Sonia.

"Is that so?" said Alec. "From what fountain of wisdom did you acquire this valuable information, my poppet?"

"Mummy told me," said Sonia.

"Ah, then there must be something in it," said Alec. "I'm just going to the pillar box. Will you come too?"

"Yes, and then I must see how the gnomes are."

"The gnomes are as well as can be expected," said Alec.

Hand in hand they walked down the path to the garden gate.

V

For some minutes Daniel Caske had lingered at Bexminster Electronics, making conversation with Robert Coppleston. He did this because he was not going to drive to his house in Abbey Street. He was going to King's Lacy and he wanted to make sure that William Carroll and Joe Major were well away before he started.

Daniel Caske, like many other clandestine lovers, was under the pathetic delusion that nobody knew about his secret attachments. And so, "Well, I must be getting home," he said to Robert Coppleston, and then he turned left at the main gates, which was the direction for Abbey Street, and, the deception accomplished as he fondly supposed, he turned left, and left, and then left again, and eventually joined the King's Lacy road on the outskirts of the city—just in time to be seen by Miss Faggott who immediately interpreted his purpose correctly and remarked upon it on the following afternoon to Mrs. Cowd when they left Morton Lodge together after the Guild committee.

"Of course," said Miss Faggott, "one didn't have to ask where he was going."

"Do you suppose Mrs. Caske knows?" asked Mrs. Cowd in a hushed voice.

"If she doesn't, I'm afraid she soon will," said Miss Faggott briskly. "I'm told he goes there nearly every day. You can't stop people talking."

Daniel Caske did not even know Miss Faggott. He was perfectly well satisfied with his strategy.

Presently he was passing the two ends of Philpot Way. "I wouldn't live there," he said to himself, "not for a king's ransom. All those ghastly women. All those farting bridge parties."

Daniel stepped on the accelerator and laughed aloud. The adjective, he thought, was particularly appropriate. He was happy in his ancient, inconvenient, and beautiful house in Abbey Street. Amy, his wife, was not. "Anyone would think we couldn't afford to live in Philpot Way," she would say. "Your meanness disgusts me." And then Daniel would look up at the Tudor ceiling in their rather dark sitting room, and tell Amy in a few choice words what he thought about Philpot Way. And Amy would say, "If my father were alive you wouldn't dare to speak to me like that. Your coarseness!" And then Daniel's cheeks would redden, and "For God's sake dry up, Amy," he would say, and pick up the newspaper. And then Amy would storm out of the room and break plates in the kitchen. And presently Daniel would get up and go out, sometimes to the club, but more often to King's Lacy to see how Janice Perriam was getting along. Janice was always pleased to see him and she never made scenes. She was always the same. That was what he liked about Janice.

What Janice particularly liked about Daniel was that he paid the rent. And other things of course. Daniel at fifty was still enormously virile.

Janice Perriam was the widow of the last Perriam in Strange, Perriam and Prosser, the King's Lacy solicitors. (There had not been a Strange since 1910.) Roland Perriam had been a golfing friend of Daniel's, and when he died at the early age of forty Daniel had helped Janice over several problems. Rather unnecessarily, old Sam Prosser had thought: if anyone were in a good position to help her it was surely he, her husband's partner. Actually Janice had been wiser than old Sam had known. She had not been left well off. It was Daniel who had made things possible for her.

Everyone in King's Lacy and in Bexminster knew about the friendship, everyone, that is, except Amy, for although Daniel took his own way he was not without a rough politeness. He never missed engagements with his wife. Even if he had quarrelled with Amy at half past four he often left Janice at precisely six forty-five on the ground that Amy would be expecting him at seven. In their strange way Amy and Daniel remained united. And so, this evening, "I've only got an hour and a half," said Daniel, "—so look lively!"

"Oh, Daniel!"

"Sorry: I must be home at a quarter past six. Amy's got people coming in for drinks. But I tell you what . . . To-morrow's the King's Lacy golf club dinner."

"Isn't Amy going?"

"No. Afterwards—on the way home—I could drop in. It's not often I can make it in the evening."

"What time, Daniel?"

"About ten."

"That's terribly late. If anyone saw you—"

"I'll be earlier if I can."

"You're not to stay later than eleven, Daniel. And don't bring the car to the house. Leave it at the Bear."

"Anything you say, sweetheart."

Daniel looked at his watch.

"Five o'clock."

Slowly, with a half-smile on his broad face, Daniel glanced round the room. There was a huge jug of delphiniums on the hearth, a bowl of roses on the sofa table, a bowl of roses on the writing-table in the window, a bowl of roses on the little French cabinet against the wall.

"Sorry I forgot to bring you any flowers."

"As if you ever have, Daniel."

Janice gave him a little kiss on the chin.

"Five o'clock and two minutes," said Daniel, glancing up at the ceiling.

"Daniel, you are awful."

"Of course," said Daniel. "That's widely understood. Don't sit there talking, girl."

At ten minutes past six he was back in Abbey Street. He even had time to post a letter before the first of Amy's guests arrived. Always Daniel Caske had everything precisely taped. But he was not, as he proudly claimed to be, a self-made man. Old Scrutt, his schoolmaster, Robert Coppleston, Philip Gossamer, even Amy, could have brought evidence to dispute that.

Saturday

I

SOME DAY SOMEONE SHOULD WRITE THE HISTORY OF THE English festival. The Three Choirs, and the Canterbury Cricket Week: and then, less sedately, the Edwardian pageants, when high society travelled great distances to see its friends disguised in farthingales, or processing as monks in some ivy-clad ruin, singing against a sky dark with impending storm. On occasion, and much to the surprise of the horses, the gentlemen had even attempted to joust. The pageants barely survived the 1914 war. The theater festivals, and then the larger music festivals, took their place. Malvern, Glyndebourne, Edinburgh, Bath, Aldeburgh, Cheltenham, Oxford, Cambridge—the British summer nowadays is one long junketing.

The King's Lacy Festival was in its fifth year, and it owed its success partly to the money of Sir Philip Gossamer, owner of Lacy Hall, the stately home just outside the town; partly to the enterprise of its director, Mrs. Manifold, who had a fascinating talent for jockeying people into doing what she wanted and making them pay for it; and partly to its conductor, Anatole Bysshe, who produced every year some operatic curiosity, which (sometimes for excellent reasons) had not been heard in the theater for a very long time. Bysshe liked to find an early work of some famous composer, preferably something which had failed at its first production, something which had subsequently been cut and altered. Then with loving care he would restore all the original music and advertise the opera as a unique opportunity of hearing what Rossini, or Balfe, or Gluck, or Dr. Arne, had really written. And opera fans from all over the country would leap at the bait and hasten down to King's Lacy to join in the fun. Sometimes, it is true, they might be heard disloyally whispering that the work was a little long and that such and such a scene (usually the one that had just been restored) might have been cut with advantage. But these were small matters. In general the King's Lacy Festival was entertaining and well done. The Corn Exchange had not been designed as an opera house, but Mrs. Manifold had spared Sir Philip no expense in remedying its defects, or in mounting her own productions. Not for Mrs. Manifold a *Figaro* in modern dress, or a magic wood expressed by two aluminum triangles and a broomstick. Mrs. Manifold always spent as much of Sir Philip's money as she possibly could, and the result was immensely rewarding, if not to Sir Philip, at least to the singers and players and producers, and to the musical public which was always happy to make the journey to what is indeed one of the most beautiful small towns in southern England.

King's Lacy is gathered around one long, broad street, divided at one end by the great church of St. Stephen, and at the other by the elegant eighteenth-century market hall.

Near the church stand the original buildings of the grammar school endowed by Edward VI, where once the boys had conducted their conversation in dog-Latin and had been warned under pain of "discreat correction," to "demeane themselves scholastick" in the streets, particularly avoiding "the rude boyes of the Towne." Today the King's School is housed in a great glass box on the outskirts of King's Lacy, and there the boys study a great deal of physics and chemistry, and never a word of the classic tongues, but probably demeane themselves scholastick in the streets no less than their predecessors.

The beautiful old school buildings now serve as offices for the Bursar and the Headmaster. Beyond them, on both sides of the street, lie unspoiled rows of Georgian shops, in places interrupted to admit a grander house of mellow brick, originally built by some citizen who had found a way of doing a little better than his neighbours. Not all of these are privately owned today. One is a bank, one (as might be expected) belongs to Strange, Perriam and Prosser, the local solicitors: but the prettiest of the houses, the one with the wisteria on it and the glimpse of the walled garden at the back, belongs to Dr. Sage, which is entirely right and proper for there has been a Dr. Sage in that house since 1820.

Halfway along High Street stands the King William Hotel, the entrance steps flanked by two great bay windows, obtruding on the pavement in that Hanoverian manner which suggests jovial repletion—and not, as it happens, untruthfully, for the King William has been modernized and at Festival time holds high state in its panelled dining room, even to the indulgence in an enormous menu card of expensive dishes; but since the guests feel safer with the *table d'hôte*, that, indeed, is all the chef reckons on preparing, deftly varying Brown Windsor with Julienne, and roast chicken with gammon and a slice of pineapple, and finishing off not merely with crème caramel and ices various but normally with a genuine fruit pie and sometimes with a lemon meringue tart. The menu is printed in an endearing mixture of English and French and on days when Dover sole is on the bill it is described as *sole au citron* as though the small slip of necessary lemon were a special treat invented by the chef for that night only. But, although the bill of fare is sometimes comical, the cooking is good, and, as is the manner of English hotels, the breakfast is large and excellent. And so everyone goes to the King William if they can, and in Festival week those who get in reckon themselves lucky, for the Bear and the Baggot Arms are small houses, and if you can't get in there it means the unlicensed Sunnyside, Graham Lodge, or even, in extremity, Balmoral, though those with cars often stay at the Angel at Bexminster, five miles away.

There is a widely held presumption among members of the local chamber of commerce that the Festival is good for trade; but it seems improbable that the visitors make any great demands upon Madame Jeanne, Hairstyles, for instance; or on Badge, Men's Outfitter & Hosier; Crumble, Fashions for Ladies; Crockett, Fancy Goods and Stationery; or Mince, Ironmonger and Radios: and none of these citizens think much of the goings-on of Festival week. Indeed Mr. Mince has been heard to describe the efforts of Anatole Bysshe as a lot of old rubbish, while Mr. Badge, who is a Plymouth Brother, has repeatedly denounced the whole festivity as devil's work. But certainly the Festival is good for the hotels and consequently for the butcher, the baker, the grocer and the fishmonger, and it retains the strong support of the proprietresses of the three tea-shops, The Marigold, The Merry Wishbone, and The Silver Teapot.

And yet it is probably the antique shops which come out

best in the end. Nearly all the visitors do a little window shopping there, and a good many of them positively enter the doors either of Mrs. Bazeley's place near the church, or of George's, the rather larger shop opposite the King William. Indeed both of them make twice as much in Festival week as in any other week of the year.

It was with a view to attracting these visitors that Mrs. Bazeley was taking so much trouble with her window display on this Saturday morning, the first day of the King's Lacy Festival. On a piece of moss green velvet lay a collection of antique jewellery which she had picked up very cheaply from an old lady and was proposing to sell at 500 percent profit. Next to the jewellery stood, or lay, a herd of curly Staffordshire sheep with that smug expression on their faces so characteristic of their kind. For the more knowing there was an imposing purple and white Rockingham tea service, and four milk white cups and saucers with a blue and gold band, which Mrs. Bazeley was prepared to describe as late Bristol, though she was well aware that they might be early New Hall. There was also a collection of Victorian fans depicting scenes from the novels of Charles Dickens. A bowl of red roses glowed in the center of the window, and darkly gleaming in the recesses of the shop were several fine tallboys and tables and looking glasses.

From the pavement Mrs. Bazeley surveyed her work with satisfaction. The bowl of roses, she thought, gave the whole thing a superior, an authentic look, was a sort of justification for the prices on the jewellery, a sort of guarantee for the Bristol-ness of those cups—besides, she persuaded herself, they very well *might* be Bristol: there was no knowing.

Mrs. Bazeley was a woman in her late fifties who contrived by the aid of makeup to look considerably older.

Makeup for Mrs. Bazeley was not a means to a glorious end, but just something that she did every day like putting on her shoes. Above her eyebrows, which were insufficiently eradicated, she painted in two brown arches: then she smacked a pink paste all over her face, dabbed two patches of red on her cheeks and fluffed a great deal of powder over the whole picture. Her nails were in the main a brilliant crimson, but as she frequently missed out some of them, the others sometimes looked as though they had been involved in an accident.

This morning the usual suggestion of incipient tuberculosis had been intensified by the use of a pale lilac lipstick. She had also done her eye shadow in brown instead of the usual blue. At a short distance Mrs. Bazeley looked very ill indeed.

She was in fact as strong as a horse, and was feeling particularly bobbish this morning owing to a series of fortunate chances which had befallen her on the previous evening. First, there had been the jewellery. Then there had been two Staffordshire figures she had picked up almost as junk in a farm house. And not only this: the old lady who parted with them was sitting in what Mrs. Bazeley instantly recognized as a genuine Chippendale wing armchair. Unfortunately the old girl was fond of it because it had belonged to her grandmother. But Mrs. Bazeley rather thought something might be done about that later on. In the meantime it made a pleasant subject for reflection. And, finally, on the way home, Mrs. Bazeley had set a seal upon her day by paying threepence less than the proper bus fare, which always pleased her very much.

"Yes," thought Mrs. Bazeley as she looked at her window, "that will do nicely." And immediately she began to wonder about George's windows, halfway along High Street.

"George, as he likes to call himself," Mrs. Bazeley used to say, for she had found out that George was a translation of Jiří, and that Mr. George's original name had been Jiří Vanásek. Mr. George made no secret of the fact that he had been born a Czech. He had every right to choose his trade name if he wanted, and he had lived in England now for twenty years: but "George, as he likes to call himself," Mrs. Bazeley would say with a little laugh, as though she could say more if she would.

The fact was that Mrs. Bazeley was jealous. Except for an occasional glance at the windows, she took no interest in "The Curio Cupboard," run by Mrs. Snaresbrook, or in "Odds and Ends" in Baggot Street, and "Treasure Trove" in Stephen's Row. They were junk shops: but George's was another matter. It was a larger shop than hers and it contained good stuff. Jiří Vanásek ("That's his real name," Mrs. Bazeley would explain) knew as much as she did about furniture, and about china he knew more. Mrs. Bazeley never scrupled to make use of Mr. George. She would often ask his opinion, particularly about continental china, but she was too jealous to admit even to herself that she ever adopted it. And so, "Yes—that will do nicely," thought Mrs. Bazeley as she looked at her window, the roses, the curly sheep, the Rockingham tea set, the Bristol (certainly Bristol) cups, and the jewellery: and immediately she wondered what Jiří Vanásek had been putting in his windows that morning. (George's had two windows. Mrs. Bazeley only had one.)

It was early yet. It seemed unlikely that there would be customers before ten. Mrs. Bazeley decided to visit the post office, which lay just beyond George's and on the same side of the road. But this was ill judged. Mrs. Bazeley had not walked twenty yards when she perceived an unexpected hazard. Madelaine Prosser had just stationed herself outside Lloyd's Bank and was joggling a collecting box up and down in a vastly irritating manner and gaily pinning oak leaves or something or other on the lapels of defenseless men emerging from the bank with pockets full of money.

With an abstracted expression on her face Mrs. Bazeley crossed the road and took refuge in Crockett's. She had suddenly remembered an urgent need for envelopes. A few minutes later, observing that Mrs. Sage was patrolling the pavement outside the King William and that Janice Perriam was picketing the post office, Mrs. Bazeley decided to go home. It was not absolutely necessary to buy stamps till Monday, she told herself, and there was so much to do in the shop. And indeed she did wisely, for Jiří Vanásek had made no alteration in his windows. There was no particular point in changing one good thing for another good thing. The left-hand window was devoted to a display of Dresden figures. The right-hand window contained a Hepplewhite bureau, a French dessert service with painted centers and rosy rims, and a great bowl of pink peonies.

The shop beyond was brighter than Mrs. Bazeley's, partly because it was larger, partly because there was more china in it. Jiří Vanásek loved beautiful things, and above all things he loved Dresden figures, Chelsea figures, and Worcester china. His tables and corner cupboards looked as though their main purpose was not to get themselves sold, but to set off the objects that they harboured or supported.

The back of the shop had been closed in to make an office, and there Jiří was sitting this Saturday morning looking at the post. There were fourteen envelopes on his table and a wrapped parcel which he had brought home on the previous evening. Five bills, eight checks, and a letter: Jiří sorted the

35

bills, sorted the checks, picked the letter up and set it down again. He knew that typewriter.

He reached out his hand for the parcel. From a great deal of wrapping he removed a lidded box. From a great deal of cotton wool packing he drew out carefully and reverently the piece he had bought at the auction yesterday. The Meissen Europa. There she sat, her garlanded hair falling across one ivory shoulder, the flush of dawn on her cheeks, her hands on the great neck of the bull, who lifted his gilded horns in triumph. Round his victorious feet flowers flamed in the grass.

It was the most lovely piece Jiří had ever bought. He doubted very much if he would ever bring himself to sell it.

For a long time he sat there, looking at it, turning it about. Presently he got up and placed it on top of a cabinet against the wall, returned to his seat and sat there gazing at it with an indulgent smile. Above it on the wall was a convex looking glass, supported on the familiar wings of a savage-looking eagle. Within the enchanted golden circle the small room swam imprisoned—Jiří, his table, the bowl of wallflowers, the sorted bills and checks, the empty envelopes, the ivory paper knife. And the one unopened letter. It would have to be opened. Jiří picked it up, turned it over, made as though to put it down again, and finally took up the paper knife and slit the envelope.

Inside it was a piece of paper and five £1 notes. Jiří looked at the paper and made a face. Then he put the notes in his wallet, pushed back his chair, got up, walked into the shop and put the paper into a lidded Worcester sugar bowl. It was something he had done before and had always hated doing. But £5, untaxed, was worth having; and anyhow, he told himself, he had no choice.

As he turned back toward the office the grandfather clock

struck eleven. Eight feet high he was and his name was Eardley Norton, London. Jiří often looked at Eardley Norton and marvelled at the joinery, the mahogany, the brass mounts. Eardley Norton was social history. He had been made for a house with a great hall, for a house with servants to clean and polish. Who was going to want him today? Eardley Norton had lived with Jiří for ten years. Jiří would be greatly troubled if anyone offered to take him away. That was the difficulty with Jiří Vanásek: he was a collector, not a tradesman.

Eleven o'clock: time for coffee. Jiří opened a door at the back of the office and stepped into his kitchen. Beyond the window a small square yard lay bright in the sunshine. All round the edge Jiří had cultivated a narrow flower bed, full now with stocks and petunias. While the kettle boiled he went out and nipped off the dead heads.

Three minutes later, when he returned to the shop, an old acquaintance was waiting for him.

"Dr. Davie!"

"None other," said Davie. "You might have expected me. I always come to the Festival, and when I come to the Festival I come to see your lovely shop. I've been poking around for some time, and I've lost my heart to those delightful yellow spill-holders with the pictures on them."

"Worcester," said Jiří.

"I guessed they were," said Davie. "Are you going to the concert this evening?"

"Yes."

"Countrymen of yours. I've never heard this Czech quartet. Are they good?"

"They say so. I haven't heard them either."

"And you? I hope you're in fine fiddle?"

This was not an inquiry after his health, as Jiři knew very well.

"I go on playing," he said. "Mostly to myself. From time to time there's a sort of orchestra here you know—and then I emerge."

"When the citizens put on *The Gondoliers*?"

"Yes. It is amusing. And how are you, sir?"

"Bouncing. I'm still at Cambridge, still talking Greek in a mild sort of way, still going to the opera, still with you in short—but coming up fast for seventy-one."

"You don't look it."

"So I like to think," said Davie, taking a peek at himself in a Queen Anne looking glass. "Heigho! Well—I must be getting along."

"One minute, sir. Would you like to see something lovely?"

"Of course I would."

Jiři beckoned Davie into the office.

"What do you think, Dr. Davie?" he said, almost in a whisper.

"It's delicious," said Davie. "Magnificent. Quite glorious. Is it—"

"Yes—it is. Meissen. From the Massingham collection. Not a flaw of any kind. You're the only person who's seen her."

"Thank you. I'm greatly honoured."

They re-entered the shop. Out in the street a man was peering through the window.

"This looks like a customer," said Davie. "You're not to sell him those yellow spill-holders. I'll be back. Goodbye."

The man on the pavement was softly humming that bit in the symphony from the New World where the triplets so cunningly pursue each other. "Music ho!" thought Davie. The next moment he was negotiating a zigzag passage between two cars and a bicycling boy going one way and a bus and another bicycling boy going the other. Dr. Davie was a born jaywalker. An aged council employee, further complicating confusion with a handcart and a broom with which he was making occasional forays into the gutter, surveyed Davie with admiration. "Well done, guv," he said. "It's as much as yer life's worth, but you done it."

Davie adored being called "guv." Unlike the facetious, impudent "squire" he felt that "guv" was intended to be polite, and that it had a lingering, acceptable flavour of hansom cabs and London in the nineties. "Guv: that's a top score," said Davie to himself, climbing the steps of the King William.

Two minutes later, embowered in a deep armchair, he was wondering how much the yellow vases were, and pondering generally on the strange ways of dealers. A coyness about prices infects them all. Either there is no ticket, or the ticket hangs with its blank side towards the window, or, if you do manage to see it, it says HF/LPT. Jiří Vanásek, Davie was thinking, was employing yet another device. Now why—but that was as far as that speculation went, because at that moment the glass door of the lounge twinkled in the sun and Richard Serpent flowed into the room. It always seemed to Davie that the solemn movements of Serpent were like the inexorable advance of an incoming tide. Behind him was Jack Pincock. Over the years, through meeting them at so many similar gatherings, Davie had got to know these two well enough to exchange a nod and a word. Serpent had been a good music critic in his time, but that in Davie's opinion was a long time ago.

"Aha!" said Serpent. "I thought you'd be here."

"Of course I am," said Davie. "I hope you've been reading it all up for our benefit"—which was a little below the belt,

39

because Serpent was well known to write his criticisms in advance with the aid of standard critical opinions. He safely discussed a work as written, not as heard. Jack Pincock, on the other hand, liked to pose as the Almighty Ear. There was never a review of his which did not castigate conductor and singers for irrational behaviour at some point or other. And as that kind of criticism can never be disproved except by a recording, Jack Pincock had a way of sounding authoritative indeed. People were often deeply chagrined to discover that they should never have enjoyed the performance of the previous evening.

"It's going to be fine for the whole week," said Serpent. "I heard the weather report on the news this morning."

"Lucky you," said Davie.

"It's usually pretty accurate," said Serpent a little defensively. He always suspected Davie of pulling his leg.

"I suppose so," said Davie, "or they wouldn't go on doing it. Have you noticed, by the way, that the people who read the meteorological announcements are specially chosen for their expert ability to say 'clouds', 'showers', 'South Downs', 'county', 'round' and 'out' with a correct cockney accent? It shows the care the authorities take, even in matters like these."

"You will come to a bad end, Dr. Davie," said Jack Pincock.

"Alas! So I have been led to expect."

Pincock and Serpent moved on to the bar. And Davie, interrupted in a thought, forgot about antique dealers and remembered the time. He heaved himself out of his chair, crossed the hall, and entered the dining room. It was a little early, but he wanted to get a table in the great bay window, delightfully trespassing on the pavement in a splendid Hanoverian bulge. One of the things Davie liked about the

King William was the absence of stuffy net curtains. From a seat in the window one could watch all the comings and goings in High Street—and that, in Davie's opinion, was one of the great minor pleasures of life. He didn't care a hang about other people peering in at him. And in fact they didn't. They were busy and moving. He was idle and seated.

There was room for two tables in the great sweep of the window. At the other one two men were already launched on their luncheon. Alice had just swept away soup plates.

"Good morning," said Davie.

"'Morning."

It was not intended as the beginning of a conversation, and anyhow the broad behind of Hilda immediately intervened, bending forward with the roast beef and Yorkshire pudding, closely followed by Alice, bearing potatoes, roast and mashed, and "garden" peas which had not long been emancipated from the deep freeze.

Davie surveyed the menu. It did not occupy him long. Roast beef was obviously the thing. And later on, equally obviously, it was lemon meringue pie. It was absurd to put up fruit salad and ices various in competition with that. He gave Alice his order, informed a local lad, disguised as a waiter, that he would like a small lager, and transferred his attention to the street.

The pavements were much less crowded now. It was everyone's lunch time. Some of the shops were closed. The bicycle boys had gone home. The road sweeper had retired from the struggle. It was not a time for window-gazing, which was perhaps why Davie noticed the man who paused outside George's. He was not looking at the things in the window. With a hand shading his eyes he was peering into the recesses of the shop. "The yellow spill-holders are not for sale," Davie murmured, and, as though he had heard him,

41

the man turned and moved slowly on along the pavement. It was the chap who had been looking into the shop an hour earlier, the man who was humming the triplets. The next time he comes back he'll surrender, thought Davie. That's the way temptation works in the antique world. But he's not going to have those yellow vases.

Alice brought the soup.

"Someone we know," said the larger of the two men at the next table. The other, a small, sandy-haired, sharp-featured man, said "Where?"

"There—outside George's."

"So it is."

Davie set down his spoon and peered across the street again. A good-looking man, somewhere in his thirties, was getting off a bicycle. This he left in an alley that ran down beside the shop. He took off his trouser clips, put them in his pocket, and paused for a minute, looking at the Dresden figures in the left-hand window. Then he entered the shop. Dimly beyond the glass Davie could see Jiří Vanásek advancing to meet him.

As Davie returned to his soup he heard the smaller man say, "That's our Robert's hobby."

"Antiques?"

"China, pottery, porcelain, whatever the right word is."

"Expensive amusement," said the big man. "Is that why he rides a push-bike?"

"I doubt if it's any more expensive than running a big car," said the other. "But you can't do both."

"Philip Gossamer does."

"I wasn't talking about the rich. *You* can't do both. Robert Coppleston can't do both. And so—"

"And so he rides a push-bike."

And then Alice arrived with the roast beef. As she left

Davie's table the big man said, "Coffee in the lounge, please, Alice."

Openly and almost mechanically he patted her on the behind. Alice took not the slightest notice.

"Yes, Mr. Caske."

"And, seeing that it's Saturday," said the sandy-haired man, "I think—"

"Two brandies," said Alice, "as usual. I'll tell Harry, Mr. Rowan."

Davie always thought it entertaining to discover things without trying. For instance "Death of Famous Star" never prompted him to buy a newspaper. The next poster would say "Death of Famous Film Star," and the next, "Death of American Star." Eventually, overlooking the stop-press in somebody's paper in the tube, he would see three lines announcing that old Flossie Farraday had passed on. The point is that in journalism "Death of Famous Star" means "Death of no longer Famous Star." If the name is really famous the poster would come out with it in the first place. So here—it was not the smallest interest to know that he had lunched next to Messrs. Caske and Rowan. But the intelligence had been vouchsafed to him. Without any effort of his a fact had been added to his store—to be tucked away in the mind along with Flossie Farraday and a lot of other useless information. Mr. Caske and Mr. Rowan—two chaps who wondered a little at "our Robert's" predilection for expensive porcelain.

The dining room was filling up now, and Davie recognized several more Festival faces. Some he would be glad to meet later on. Some not—not Mrs. Mapleton-Morley, for instance, who was fortunately seated at this moment in a far corner of the room, attended as usual by her famous niece, with the

43

dubious auburn hair. But a time for speaking would in-
evitably arrive.

Richard Serpent and Jack Pincock were studying the
menu at a table near the door. "Mark my words," said Pincock, as Davie passed them on the way out, "yours will be
one of the first heads to roll." And how like little Pincock,
thought Davie. He makes a mild joke and it goes well. So he
has to make it again half an hour later. Or am I a hypercriti-
cal old beast? I expect so.

The hall was empty but the glass door to the lounge was
slowly squeezing itself shut with the slow assistance of
compressed air. Davie noticed that because it always irritated him. Doors, he felt, should shut at once and not obey
the whim of some ghostly contrivance.

Designing a short stroll before lying down, he got his hat
from the row of pegs which serves as a cloak room at the
King William, and stood for a moment contemplating the
mass of overlapping information on the hotel notice board—
the Festival announcements, the cinema, the services at St.
Stephen's, the county gardens open to the public last week
and next week but not this week, a couple of stately homes
(one with teas 2/6), Madame Jeanne, Hairstyles, and a
bazaar to be opened on Tuesday, no, last Tuesday, by the
Countess of Dagenham.

Behind him in a telephone box a man was saying in a
confidential voice, but not quite confidential enough for the
inadequate defenses of the King William telephone boxes, "I
don't want to take it to Sir Philip or Mr. Rowan without
being certain. If I'm wrong I'd look a fool . . . Thank you,
Mr. Carroll. I'll come right away."

Davie glanced towards the glass door of the lounge. If the
speaker didn't want to run into Mr. Rowan, he was thinking . . . and then he heard the door of the telephone box

snick behind him and the man walked quickly to the front door. Reminded of his stroll, Davie followed him.

II

Robert Coppleston had not got away as early as he had intended.

"So this is your day off," Mrs. Coppleston had said at breakfast. "And the poor old lawn will have to wait." She had been thinking it over in the night watches. After all, the concert at Lacy wasn't till the evening.

"I can do it tomorrow."

"I'd rather you didn't do it on Sunday, Robert. It doesn't look well. Never mind. It doesn't really matter." She lifted the purple cozy from the octagonal teapot—a familiar mid-conversational gambit of hers. "I was only thinking that I have to give tea to the committee this afternoon—the Guild, you know. Mrs. Cowd is such a devoted gardener. And so is Miss Faggott. It would have been rather nice if—"

"I'll do it before I go, then," said Robert.

"Oh no, Robert—you mustn't do that, dear. It would spoil your day."

"No—it's all right. I can manage. It won't take long."

"I never meant—"

"It's all right, Mother."

"If you're quite sure, dear—"

Mrs. Coppleston poured herself a second cup of tea. She had earned it. Neither of them had altered by a shade the happy tone of voice which always prevailed at Morton Lodge, especially at breakfast time, and yet a duel had been fought, which had as usual been won by Mrs. Coppleston. Robert knew that he could win every time if he chose to be

45

firm—but somehow it never seemed to be the necessary moment for firmness. Truly, it did not matter in the least whether he arrived at Roughton at eleven or at noon—so why not be obliging?

In the end it was already one o'clock when he reached King's Lacy and Roughton was three miles further on. He decided to change his plans. Merry's must wait. Instead he called at George's.

"I thought it was about time I saw you," said Jiří Vanásek.

"I'm going to Witherby this afternoon. The garden's open. So I thought I'd call in on the way. And tonight I'm going to the concert at Lacy. Are you?"

"Yes."

"I thought you would be, seeing it's a Czech affair."

Robert glanced round the shop.

"Anything good?"

"Lots good, lots—but I don't know that it's for you. There's nothing new in Staffordshire."

"I like that Dresden in the window."

"I didn't know Dresden was your line."

"Only because I can't afford it," said Robert. "I love it. I'm going to afford it some day."

"Come here," said Jiří. "I'll show you something to dream about."

Robert followed him into the office. Europa and her glorious Bull seemed to fill the little room with light.

"It's fantastic, Jiří. The loveliest thing I ever saw."

"It's the loveliest thing ever made," said Jiří. "Really, I do think so. I got it yesterday at an auction."

For a minute they stood side by side in solemn admiration. Then, "I'm just running up some lunch in the kitchen," said Jiří. "Join me."

"Thanks very much."

"Have a look round. I'll call you when I'm ready. I don't suppose anyone will come in, but if so give a yell."

For several minutes Robert moved around the shop. Those yellow vases were attractive. And the small tureen standing on its own dish: the deepest blue with gold decorations and white medallions filled with fruit and birds and roses. Robert wondered if anyone had ever used the thing. Would anyone ever dare to use it?—actually dare to spoon out bread sauce, say, for it wasn't big enough for soup. As a practical object for the dinner table, short of serving an Empress upon bended knee, it was as delightfully improbable as it was deliciously pretty.

On the other hand he would risk using that gold and white tea service. People always jabbered about modern improvements in hygiene. It was curious that no one ever made a lidded sugar bowl these days—at least not a porcelain one: there were those tin things one saw in restaurants: but in good china it wasn't thought necessary now, that obvious hygienic defense belonging to the bad old days.

Robert Coppleston lifted the lid. A few seconds later carefully and slowly he replaced it. That much his love for beautiful things made certain. But his face was red and his hands were trembling. He had suddenly discovered a great need to telephone to someone for advice, and it was certainly not possible to use George's telephone.

After a moment's hesitation he went to the back of the shop and opened the kitchen door.

"Jiří! Please forgive me. I've suddenly remembered something. I can't stay. Sorry!"

"Hey!" said Jiří, setting down his omelet pan. "What's the matter? . . ."

47

For answer the shop bell rang and stopped again. Robert had gone.

"Silly ass!" said Jiří. "Now there's twice too much to eat."

III

Robert Coppleston crossed the road, ran up the steps of the King William, and went straight to one of the telephone boxes at the far end of the hall.

"Can I speak to Mr. Carroll, please? Is he in?"

"Who is it speaking, please?"

It was the prim voice of some elderly female servant.

"Coppleston—Robert Coppleston."

"Will you wait a moment, please."

It was a long time longer than a moment, but at last he heard William Carroll say, "Coppleston? You wanted me?"

"Yes, Mr. Carroll, please."

"Well? What about?"

"I've just found something, Mr. Carroll. It looks important to me."

"What do you mean—*looks* important?"

"I don't want to say too much on the telephone, Mr. Carroll."

"Perhaps not. But say something."

"It's a paper I've found—a message, I think."

"Something to do with the firm?"

"I'm sure it is, and I'm afraid it's important."

"Where are you?"

"King's Lacy—the King William."

"And where did you find this paper?"

Robert hesitated. Then he said in a low voice, "At George's, across the road."

"Have you got a car?" asked Carroll.

48

"No—I'm on a push-bike."

"That will mean how long?"

"Fifteen minutes. Fifteen minutes, easy."

"All right. It's a gardening day for me. Sarah will show you where I am. Or come to the rose garden if you know where that is. Then we can discuss whatever it is—and perhaps you'll stay to tea."

"Thank you, Mr. Carroll."

"One thing—why have you chosen me for this confidence?"

Robert Coppleston knew why, but it was difficult to explain. He just said "I thought you'd be best, Mr. Carroll. I don't want to take it to Sir Philip or Mr. Rowan without being certain. If I'm wrong I'd look a fool."

"See you in about twenty minutes."

"Thank you, Mr. Carroll. I'll come right away."

Robert Coppleston rang off and stood for a moment cautiously looking out of the round window in the door. A rather more than middle-aged gentleman was studying the announcements on the notice board. He could see no one else. Robert let himself out and made straight for the front door. And Davie, who had had enough of the announcements, put on his soft green hat and followed him. Why a "snap brim," by the way? He always wondered about that but could never remember to investigate the problem when actually engaged in buying one. It was very curious.

Standing on the steps of the King William and pondering this problem of haberdashery, Davie became aware that the man who had just left the hotel was the owner of the bicycle parked in the alley beside George's shop, the man the other two had talked about at lunch. He had just mounted and was about to ride down the street in the direction of St. Stephen's; and Davie, who had a mind to take a look at Mrs.

Bazeley's window, set off in the same direction. The last he saw of him the cyclist was neatly passing the crossroads just ahead of a red light.

The cars came to a stop, and so did Davie. He wanted to peer into a flower shop. And after that at a shop deliriously described as a "second hand boutique"; *sic transit* the ordinary meaning of language, thought Davie. Three lights later, when he reached the crossroads himself, a fat furniture van was waiting at the top of the queue. Immediately behind it was an Aston-Martin, and Davie recognized the driver. It was the small sandy man the waitress had called Mr. Rowan. He was glaring at the furniture van as though he were in an angry hurry. But his apparent purpose was pleasure. There was a golf bag on the seat beside him, and he was heading in the direction of the King's Lacy links.

IV

On the road to the King's Lacy golf course a signpost on the left—possibly dating from the nineteenth century, so old it looks—is marked Combe Magna, and though its ancient arm points crazily to the ground, the traveller who ventures down the lane will in time arrive at the village. And half a mile before he gets there he will pass the gate of Combe Court. The rhododendron drive had been there when William Carrroll bought the place, but most of the beautiful garden within he had created with the aid of Henry Badge (younger brother of Badge, Men's Outfitter, High Street, King's Lacy) and two young men who were under Mr. Badge's discipline.

The house, a charming Regency affair, stands on the side of a hill, its gardens sloping down like the hanging gardens of Babylon to the brook at the bottom of the valley. But the hill that rises on the other side of the brook—and this is what one sees from the house—has not been interfered with by man for two hundred years, not since the planting of the hedges, and the beech trees on the skyline.

William Carroll had been drinking coffee, and contemplating this venerable scene, when Sarah stepped on to the verandah and informed him that he was wanted on the telephone.

"Drat the telephone, Sarah."

Sarah was not going to smile, but that was exactly what she thought herself. Nasty, dangerous thing. She always held the earpiece two inches away from her head as though she feared it would get entangled in her hair or do her a mischief of some sort. Reliably she made gay work of names and messages.

"A Mr. Cobblestone, sir."

"Cobblestone?"

"That's what he said, sir."

"Cobblestone—must be Coppleston. All right, Sarah—I'll go."

"Thank you, sir," said Sarah, pleased that she would not have to approach the thing again with a message for a strange man.

Coppleston had not wanted to say much, and he certainly hadn't. Beyond the fact that he had found something at George's which concerned Bexminster Electronics, there was nothing so far to consider, and Mr. Carroll, who had a cool and logical mind, decided to waste no time on speculation. So he finished his coffee and then ambled through the library to the hall and looked for Sarah.

"Sarah—there's a Mr. Coppleston coming to see me from King's Lacy. He's on a push-bike and he says it will take him fifteen minutes. It would take me about an hour, but I suppose he knows best."

"I expect so, sir."

"I'm not going to waste time hanging around. I'll be in the rose garden. He may find his way there on his own, but if he comes to the house will you please show him the way."

"Very good, sir."

"We'll come back for tea. On the terrace. Four thirty, please."

The rose garden was some way from the house. Indeed, it was rather nearer to the gate. But it lay behind the screen of rhododendrons, and Carroll rather doubted if Robert Coppleston would find his way there. He'd have to go up to the house and back again. What with one thing and another he hardly expected to see him for at least half an hour, which might be time enough to review the damaged pergola and consider what Badge should do about it. With a mind full of roses and Albertine in particular, he set off down the gravel path.

And yet a mind not entirely full of roses. What on earth was Coppleston doing in George's? he was thinking. He knew he was interested in gardens. That was a proper and normal hobby for a company's secretary. He probably took a pride in mowing the lawn. But china and Chippendale? Those were expensive and frangible delights.

Mr. Carroll sat down on a stone seat and contemplated his roses. Peace, Iceberg, Grace of Monaco, June Park, Oberon, Nymph, Albertine. They were lovely but he wished so many of the old roses had not disappeared. When did you last see La France? Or the Seven Sisters? Those pale pink clusters he remembered as a boy, climbing the vicarage wall—where were they now? It was an idle speculation. One might as well ask when did you last see your great-grandmother? Flowers have an ancestry as well as people.

It was very quiet. Except for a cuckoo shouting away in the distance there was really no sound at all. It might have been a hundred and fifty years ago, so far it seemed removed from modern busyness. Two butterflies made arabesques above the flowers. There was no other movement.

Then, in the lane, a hundred yards away, a car drove past the gate. But either it stopped or suddenly moved beyond hearing: for again the garden was utterly still except for the butterflies and in the distance that persistent cuckoo.

"Enough of nothing," said William Carroll to himself. He got up and advanced on the pergola.

It was past four o'clock when he returned to the house, and "Well? Didn't the man come?" he asked Sarah.

"No, sir. I thought perhaps he'd gone to the rose garden, as you said he might."

"He did not. It's an extraordinarily odd thing. He rang to ask if he could come, and said he'd be here in fifteen minutes."

"He might have had an accident—or a puncture, sir. I expect it was a puncture," said Sarah, seeming pleased at her immediate grasp of alternative solutions.

"Why didn't he telephone? He *must* have had an accident. It's the only explanation."

Later, in his bath, he remembered that Coppleston had told Philip Gossamer he was going to the concert. He might have seen me there, he thought—why all that fuss? But perhaps not: it could have been difficult.

But William Carroll never wasted time on things temporarily insoluble. He turned off the hot tap with his big toe, scrubbed the roses out of his fingernails and lay back in the water. Considering he was turned forty-five, he thought his brown lean body was still rather beautiful.

Half an hour later there was smoked salmon and white wine in the library. There would be more wine and food of a sort at Lacy in the interval. It was one of those three guinea affairs. Music and grub. The two together are alleged to invoke the Festival spirit.

V

Dr. Davie and Lady Meade-Fuller were early arrivals at Lacy. They met in the antechamber to the great salon.

"I felt sure we could count on you, Mildred."

"My dear R.V.," said Lady Meade-Fuller, "what a delightful surprise! I must say I like your tie."

"Do you? It was chosen after long and anxious deliberation in the King's Road, Chelsea."

"Still a prey to vanity, R.V.?"

"Certainly. Vanity may be the pursuit of emptiness, but it's what makes the world a possible place to live in. Without vanity we'd all look like neolithic man."

"What a fascinating thought!" said Mildred Meade-Fuller, glancing past Davie's shoulder towards the door. People were coming in and she liked to have immediate intelligence of new arrivals.

"Just think of the first neolithic girl to run a comb through her hair," Davie went on, "and the others muttering 'vag sug,' meaning 'vain slut,' and then slowly realizing that the young men were taking more notice of the creature than of them. It would have been about then that they started boiling up whortleberries to make lipstick."

"You know too much about these things, R.V.," said Mil-

54

dred Meade-Fuller, simultaneously bowing to a passing stranger, and adding, "Oh dear! I thought I knew that man."

"You will, Mildred, I don't doubt," said Davie.

Lady Meade-Fuller raised her eyebrows. "Really, R.V.!" she said in a loud whisper, "These skirts! One doesn't know which way to look."

"I would have thought one did," said Davie.

And now, threading their way through the crowd, and bent upon reaching Lady Meade-Fuller, Davie observed three lady patrons of the arts, screaming a great deal about "dear Mildred." Inevitable that they should be there, but not inevitable, thought Davie, that he should have to talk to them. He eased himself into a corner and surveyed the throng of loud-voiced ladies and gentlemen baying for music or perhaps merely seeking a social diversion in beautiful surroundings. And beautiful they were—this house, created in the noblest eighteenth-century taste, with inlaid panelled walls and coffered ceilings of infinite elegance. Around the walls depended pictures of Gossamers dead and gone. Glass cabinets in the corners displayed Sir Philip's famous collection of Bow and Chelsea figures. And here, among all this beauty, here they all were, the old familiar faces—Serpent, Pincock, Lady Boston, Miss Myrtle and Lady Cranberry, twin souls of the opera house, and Frederick Dyke, that prize eccentric, standing concealed, so far as he could manage it, behind a statue of Apollo and looking, as he so commonly did, like a spy in a play about the Congress of Vienna. Frederick Dyke was an added pleasure to any musical gathering.

And there, with Miss Bangle in support, was Mrs. Mapleton-Morley; she had succeeded in cornering Lady Gossamer. Sir Philip, Davie noted with admiration, had managed to shake hands and pass himself on to the next comer with the skill of an ambassador. Davie was sorry for Miss Bangle. She was the traditional niece of the case books, patronized and put upon. She would be an elderly spinster by the time she inherited what Mrs. Mapleton-Morley had to leave: if she did inherit it. Mrs. M. often insinuated that in certain circumstances she might be induced to leave her money to the Poor Ladies' Association. But Miss Bangle was making a fight of it. Davie couldn't help admiring her sprightly demeanour and the way she kept her hair the same roaring chestnut. If Miss Bangle had ever had the time to inveigle a passing bachelor she would have left Mrs. Mapleton-Morley flat, and serve her right. The pity was that it was never possible to talk to Miss Bangle without getting involved with Mrs. Mapleton-Morley, and the prospect of that defeated even Davie's charity.

He made a strategical move towards the concert room.

As yet it was almost empty and he walked round the room, studying the pictures. Most of them were large pictures of a lady in a garden with a background of distant trees, and each of them wore a skirt which could not have been taken into a garden, not at any time of year. It was one of the problems of history, Davie reflected. Did women ever look like their pictures? Did Madame Suggia, for instance? If they did, it was because the pictures were not good. But the clothes! He returned to the clothes: they could not have been trailed along the garden path, they could not have been managed in the park. The picture of Lady Honoria Gossamer in the character of Diana was admittedly a fantasy. But no less a fantasy was Caroline, wife of Sir George Gossamer, who had apparently been picking strawberries in a dress which would have graced a royal birthday.

On one side of the dais at the end of the room an arrangement of screens provided a green room for the artists. Davie stood beside it, studying a group of Tudor children rigidly encased in clothes from ear to heel. And was *that* true? he was thinking. How did boys fight each other in ruffles?

And then, on the other side of the screen, a man spoke— quickly, emphatically, softly. It meant nothing to Davie, but as he turned away he caught three words in the flow of foreign sounds, three names—Bazeley, George's, Vanásek. In a way it was surprising—but George's was a likely object of interest for Czech visitors. The voice continued. Davie moved on to inspect Sir Francis Gossamer, who was less unreasonably clad than the ladies for a shooting expedition in the park.

Outside the door a footman beat upon a gong. It was the signal for the company to stop screaming and to find their places. Davie made his way to his seat, and fished out his program. Dvořák, Beethoven, Interval, Brahms, Janáček.

Janáček . . . Vanásek. Come to think of it, the name had seemed to invoke in the speaker behind the screen an urgent and almost conspiratorial excitement. Central Europeans were so serious about everything. (And so often had had good cause to be.) Which of them, he pondered, had been talking to whom about Mrs. Bazeley and Jiří?

And now, here they were, Dalibor Kalaš, 1st violin, Milan Horácek, 2nd violin, Antonin Borský, viola, and Rudolf Turek, cello. They stood in a line and bowed without smiling. Smiles were for later. Then they sat down, adjusted their chairs by centimeters, and made the painful preliminary noises of final tuning.

At that moment of suspense most of the audience were probably looking at the beautiful Dalibor Kalaš, waiting for his secret nod to the other three. But Davie had unexpectedly found the answer to his question. He was looking at the cellist. The man who had been peering into Jiří's window earlier that day had certainly been Rudolf Turek.

VI

Fifty minutes later the players were on their feet, bowing and smiling. Then they left the platform and immediately returned again with suitable expressions on their faces of mingled gratitude and humility—a pleasant, almost Chinese, convention which deceives no one—and after the audience had given the quartet to understand that any natural anxiety they might have felt about the quality of their performance was entirely groundless, they retired again, the applause died down abruptly, and the company arose rather more as one man than is usual, for the point was that no one was unmindful of the fact that the tickets—three guineas—included wine, red and white, salmon mayonnaise, éclairs and coffee. No one wanted to be seen to be greedy; but no one meant to be left behind; and so they arose as one man; they would neither be forward nor backward in this matter. That is to say most of them wouldn't be. Fat old Prebendary Furston always took a seat by the door for the express purpose of gaining the best possible start, and a certain anxiety clouded even the best bred faces when they realized that they were in a disadvantageous position and were going to be last out of the room.

Davie found himself pushing through the door beside Frederick Dyke.

"I perceive a light of battle in your eye, Dyke," he said.

"What you see," said Dyke in his severe and scholarly voice, "is the light of bottle. Perhaps we may meet at the opera next week in less agitating circumstances. At the moment—" and Frederick Dyke disappeared in the surge of bodies pressing forward as politely as possible in pursuit of their money's worth.

In the supper room William Carroll was hovering near Sir Philip. Perceiving which, Sir Philip extricated himself from a conversation of civility by smartly introducing two old acquaintances to each other, and in the resulting confusion turning aside to meet Carroll.

"It was good, wasn't it?"

"Splendid—but where's our secretary?"

"Secretary?"

"Yes—Coppleston."

"Ah—yes," said Sir Philip, but without enthusiasm. A friendly remark at a board meeting was not intended to be too closely interpreted. "Isn't he here?"

"I don't think so. And I'll tell you a rather odd thing. He rang up this afternoon and asked if he could come to see me. He was worried about something or other. He said he'd come right away. But he didn't. And he said he was coming tonight. But he hasn't. It looks as though our secretary might have had an accident."

"I hope not."

"I shall ring up his home tomorrow and find out."

"Do. Coppleston's a good chap. I hope you'll join us for a drink later. The Czechs will be there. I'm driving them into King's Lacy afterwards. Excuse me, William. I must have a word with that old bird over there." And Sir Philip Gossamer moved into the fray, intent on performing a politeness. His attentions meant nothing at all, except that he was an excellent host.

Carroll remained back to the wall, a removed spectator of four hundred people stowing it away. Davie noticed him as he came in, commending the nobly cut blue suit, the light blue tie, the pale blue handkerchief with the dark blue edge.

Davie enjoyed that sort of thing. Lean and tall and dark, William Carroll was a very noticeable person.

As soon as he had collared a drink and something to eat Davie made his way through the crowd to where Jiří Vanásek was standing alone in a corner.

"I saw you from afar," he said. "You're all on your own."

"I don't know any of these people," said Jiří—"and it makes one feel stupid. I was expecting someone, but he isn't here, so I'm a bit lost."

"Your Czech friends were good."

"Yes."

"Are you going round to speak to them afterwards?"

"Good gracious, no!"

"It might not be amiss," said Davie. "I heard one of them talking about you before the concert began."

"Talking about *me!*" said Jiří, his glass suddenly arrested halfway towards his mouth. "What—what was he saying?"

"How do I know? Czechs talk Czech—but I heard your name and also Mrs. Bazeley's. Perhaps one of them went shopping at Mrs. Bazeley's and she informed him that there was another shop run by one of their countrymen."

"Perhaps. But nobody did come to my place."

"You're wrong," said Davie. "Do you remember the chap who was looking through your window this morning when I was leaving your shop?"

"I didn't notice him."

"He was Turek, the cellist."

"He didn't come in," said Jiří. "No one came in. No one like that, I mean."

"Are you feeling all right?" asked Davie.

Jiří Vanásek had suddenly gone very pale.

"Yes, thank you. But it's hot in here."

"Did you come up on the bus?"

"Yes."

"I was very lordly and hired a car. May I give you a lift home?"

"I'd be most grateful."

Outside the door the footman banged on the gong.

"Time to go back," said Davie. "Sure you're all right?"

"Yes, thank you."

"We'll meet in the hall, then."

And now the audience were all turned towards the door. Or most of them were. On the return journey Prebendary Furston could afford to dawdle. He helped himself to another glass of Beaujolais, and a final éclair marooned by a happy chance on an empty plate at the back of the table. It seemed a pity to leave it. He was smiling as he sailed back to the hall. It had just occurred to him that he was an excellent illustration of the Biblical apothegm "the first shall be last."

He reached his seat very conveniently as the quartet stepped onto the platform.

Jiří Vanásek had also chosen the back row, but not for the same reason. He had come to the concert a little for the music, a little for the occasion, but mostly because he wanted to make sure that Dalibor Kalaš was really Dalibor Kalaš. He had thought himself secure. It was wholly disquieting to realise that Dalibor Kalaš might also have had a determination to scrutinize Jiří Vanásek. And equally disquieting was another thought that weaved itself crisscross with the first. Where the devil was Robert Coppleston? It wasn't a small thing at all to accept an invitation to lunch and ten minutes later to disappear without a word of explanation. And it wasn't a small thing at all that Robert should not be at the concert. He'd bought a ticket. He'd certainly meant to come. But he wasn't there. And Dalibor Kalaš was.

Jiří Vanásek heard nothing of the Brahms or the Janáček. He was ahead even of Prebendary Furston at the cloakroom. But Davie had not been so well placed for escape. It meant waiting. Jiří went outside and stationed himself in the shadow of an elaborately clipped yew. He feared he had made a mistake in accepting the invitation. He might have got away sooner in one of the coaches waiting at the side of the gravel sweep. Beyond, the lights of the earliest leavers already streaked across the park towards moonlit lanes.

Then Davie appeared in the doorway and Jiří stepped up to him.

"Ah—there you are," said Davie. "I was afraid I'd lost you. We're over here."

He had waited too long. Behind Davie in the hall three of the Czech musicians were making bows of politeness at Lady Gossamer. The fourth, Rudolf Turek, the cellist, was staring through the open door. Perhaps he was looking at the rectangle of summer night. But it seemed to Jiří Vanásek that he looked at him, standing in the spotlight of the great lantern that hung from the porch.

VII

"Daniel," said Janice Perriam, "I wish you hadn't come. I should have said no. And now that you are here you're like an old bear. What's the matter?"

"I can't help being a bear: I thought you liked my being a bear."

"I like your being a teddy bear—not an angry old bear: that's quite different. If you're not going to—to make yourself interesting—"

Daniel laughed at that.

"Interesting! That's a splendid word for it. I'm sorry,

sweetheart. I said I'd come, and I wanted to see you: but I'm tired. I've had a day."

"'A day'—on a Saturday?"

"It was all right till lunch time and then everything went wrong. First I had some bad news—and then I was late at the golf club—and there was a muddle over the matches, and I lost my temper."

"I've heard about your temper, Daniel. It's a great mistake to lose your temper. It takes years off your life."

"I jolly nearly took forty years off that fool secretary's life."

"And then?"

"And then I found we were supposed to wear dinner jackets, and I had to go back and change."

"And then?"

"And then they put me between Colonel Bummage—"

"Daniel."

"Bummage, Rummage, Rammage—I don't know—and Skeat, the silly little curate at St. Cecilia's. Skeat never said a word except may I offer you the parsnips or some damned vegetable or other, and Bummage told one anecdote which lasted through three hilarious courses."

"And in the end it's I who gets the benefit. You ought to be getting some compensation for all your troubles and bad temper, but—"

"Now don't you start irritating me, Janice."

"All right, Daniel. Have a drink and go home. But please be careful. Don't bang the door, and do listen for anyone in the road before you let yourself out."

"Sorry I'm so put about, Janice, but I think you're right. And anyway it's twenty-five to eleven."

And so Daniel said goodnight to Janice, and somehow, in the end, took twenty minutes saying it.

"Eleven o'clock, Daniel," whispered Janice. "Darling Daniel, I'm so glad you stayed to say goodnight."

"I hope I made myself 'interesting,' sweetheart."

Janice giggled. "Yes, Daniel. You know you did. But you *must* go now, and don't forget about the door, and please be careful when you let yourself out."

And so at five minutes past eleven Daniel Caske paused on the doorstep of the house in Baggot Avenue, and listened. In the garden he paused again, looking to right and left across neat hedges of Japanese honeysuckle, and escalonia, the moon-tipped spears of delphinium, the congregations of roses. Then he walked softly down the path, quietly opened the gate, and stepped onto the pavement as gently as a shadow. He was doing what Janice had asked of him, and yet, if anyone had seen him indulging in these elaborate precautions, what would they have thought? But nobody did see him, and Daniel Caske walked swiftly on, turned to the right and entered the lower end of Brook Lane.

Brook Lane runs parallel to High Street; beside it a brook, and beyond the brook a row of rosy brick houses, each with its small front garden, each with its bridge across the water. The fluorescence of High Street is diminished in Brook Lane. There are only two public lights, one near each end. In the street between the moon does duty.

Halfway along the lane, the alley at the side of George's shop slopes up to connect Brook Lane with High Street. In the house opposite the end of the alley, the house that faced Jiří Vanásek's back wall, lived Joe Major.

Daniel Caske glanced at his watch, crossed Joe Major's bridge over the brook, opened the garden gate, walked up the path and opened the front door. "Joe!" he called softly, and as there was no answer he walked down the passage and tapped on the door on the left. No reply. Daniel Caske opened the door and peeped inside. The room was bright in the moonlight, but there was certainly no one at home.

Daniel Caske entered, shut the door behind him, walked over to the clock on the mantelshelf and compared his watch with it. For a minute he waited. Then glancing again at his watch he let himself out, walked quietly down the path, crossed the bridge and crossed the lane. His way to the Bear car park lay up the alley by Jiří Vanásek's shop, where the close walls echo indeed if you walk between them with a resolute tread, but not if you walk softly. Daniel was walking softly, presumably as a sort of hangover from Janice's anxious caution. He had walked softly since he left her house, and now in the alley beside George's shop he walked more than softly, for he could hear voices over the wall. The voice of Mr. Vanásek and some visitor. Daniel Caske stopped to listen, and the voice in the garden stopped at the same time, as though, embarrassingly, it had stopped to listen to Daniel Caske.

He did not continue on his way till the voice on the other side of the wall began to speak again.

VIII

As the chimes of St. Stephen's were striking half past ten the hired car had deposited Davie and Jiří Vanásek before the steps of the King William. It was St. Stephen's last pronouncement for the night: by a merciful decree he would not startle the silence again till seven o'clock in the morning. Other cars were dropping other Festival visitors both at the King William and farther down the street at the Bear and the Baggot Arms. The pavements of King's Lacy, usually quiet at this time of night, were loud with people saying goodnight to each other in that jolly high-pitched voice peculiar to night revellers.

"See you tomorrow, darling."

"It was a lovely concert."

"Goodnight."

"Sleep well."

And bang went the car doors for the special benefit of those citizens who had retired to sleep at their usual hour.

Davie said, "Can I persuade you to come in for a drink?"

"I was going to ask if you'd come to my place," said Jiří, and, as Davie hesitated, he added, "I'd be glad if you would, Dr. Davie."

Davie could not be sure about the pallor of Jiří Vanásek. The fluorescent lighting of this age makes everyone look moribund. But he had looked pale earlier in the evening, and he had said "I'd be glad" as though he wanted to say "I'd be thankful."

And so, "May I do that?" Davie said. "I'd like to, very much."

Jiří led the way down the narrow alley at the side of George's shop. Near the bottom a gate in the wall led into a small yard, squared with flowers—Jiří's garden—one side in shadow, the other bright in the moonlight.

"What a marvellous smell!" said Davie. "Tobacco plant."

"Yes. Come in, Dr. Davie. Two steps. Now—what will you have? Whisky?"

"Please, yes—with water."

It was a warm and beautiful night. "Shall we sit outside?" said Jiří. He put the light out in the kitchen, and brought out two chairs. "The moon's enough."

For half a minute neither of them spoke. Then Jiří said, "Dr. Davie—I want to tell you something."

"I rather thought you did," said Davie.

"It's a long story."

"Very well."

It was an hour later when Davie rose to go.

"Come through the shop," said Jiří. "It will be easier for you."

"May we say goodnight to Europa as we pass?"

Jiří opened the office door and put the light on.

"I understand your delight. She is very beautiful."

There was no need of a light in the shop. A lamp post just to the side of the window cast its ghastly beam along the polished surfaces, and like pale ghosts Davie and Jiří crossed the shop to the door.

"I'm so glad you're not so ill as you look," said Davie.

"Thank you for listening to all my talk."

"Indeed, no: thank you for confiding in me, and thank you for my drink."

Jiří stood by the open door and watched his visitor mount the steps of the King William. Then he shut and locked the door and moved back towards the patch of light that lay like a carpet outside the office door. By the Worcester tea service, gleaming in the sallow light from the street, he stopped, lifted the lid of the sugar bowl, and peered inside. There was nothing there. That was how he liked it to be. He did not want to know which of his customers was involved in this business.

He put the lid back and moved on to the kitchen. He was ready for bed. Without putting on the light he shut the back door. But before bolting it he remembered that the light was still on in the office. He went to put it out, altered his mind, shut the door, and sat down at his table. He felt utterly exhausted.

On the opposite wall he saw himself in the convex looking

glass, the room floating round him like an enchantment. He told himself that, in such a glass, the door might open—and yet not open behind him, that the glass might reflect things not there. Like a child, he often frightened himself with thoughts like that, born of anxiety and loneliness.

He lowered his eyes and sat staring at his blotting pad. Presently he picked up the paper knife and laid its cool flat ivory against his cheek. He had told Dr. Davie a story he had never told anyone else, and now he was telling it to himself all over again.

And lying awake in his dark bedroom on the other side of the street, Dr. Davie was pondering the same story, thought for thought. Prague, 1944, twenty-five years ago.

IX

Jiří's bed was in the corner of the living room. Sometimes he would wake up and see his mother sitting in the candle-light. He never made a sound. He liked to watch her shadow knitting enormous socks against the wall. And presently he would fall asleep again without her knowing he had been awake.

If his father were in the room his parents would talk softly together, partly because they did not want to wake Jiří, partly because people did speak softly in Prague in 1944. Usually he did not hear, but there was one night when his mother's voice was raised a little. "Do not bring the boy into this, Ivo," she was saying. "There is trouble enough. He is too young."

"Someone young is needed," said Ivo Vanásek.

Jiří heard that, but it made no sense to him lying half awake in the light of a distant candle. In the silence that followed he thought perhaps that his mother was crying. He

68

was sorry for that, but while he was thinking of what he would like to give her as a present, he fell asleep.

He was twelve.

Three days later his father told him what he had to do.

It was quite simple. On the coming Saturday he was to ride his bicycle to a certain place and park it against the fence near a pile of rubble and old cars. It was to be there at half past three, no earlier, no later, and then he was to walk to the church of St. Thomas. When he got there he would find his bicycle parked in the little alley at the side of the church. If it was not there he was to go away for ten minutes and return, but he was only to return once. If the bicycle was there he was to ride straight home. If it wasn't he was to come home as soon as he could.

That evening Jiří and his father went for a walk together. With a jerk of his thumb Ivo Vanásek showed him the exact places he needed to remember.

"You must do it right, Jiří. It isn't a game. It's a matter of somebody's life."

"Is it against the Germans?" Jiří whispered.

Ivo Vanásek slightly inclined his head. For good measure he nodded amiably to a passing policeman.

"You don't need to know anything more, Jiří, and the less you know the better."

("That is the usual theory behind secret undertakings," said Jiří Vanásek to Dr. Davie. "But it isn't entirely true. It is possible to know too little."

("Yes," said Davie. "Certainly it is.")

At twenty-five past three on that afternoon Jiří mounted his bicycle and rode to the fence by the rubbish dump. It seemed easy what he had to do, but suppose someone saw him and asked him what he was doing—what would he say? It seemed silly to leave a bicycle in such a place. But when he got to the fence and looked around him he saw the point. There was no one about. The site across the road was a ruin, the shell of a house which had been destroyed in a fire. There was no one to watch him from those ghostly window frames.

He left the bicycle just inside the fence, crossed the road, and started to walk up the street nearly opposite the dump. Still there was no one about, but when he turned to the left some fifty yards along the street, he saw a German patrolman waiting at the next corner. Jiří walked on, looking neither to right nor left. If he were stopped he was to say he was going to see his grandmother. He could see the big man looking at him. He felt sure he was going to ask him his business.

And then, suddenly, not far away, somewhere behind him and to the right, came the sound of a car backfiring, and then again, and then a screech of wheels like the sound of an accident. Laying a hand on his revolver, the patrolman crossed the road and looked down a side street in the direction of the noise. This was something more interesting than a small boy out for a walk. Besides, was it a car backfiring? Could it have been a shot?

Jiří kept on walking. Then, away to his left he heard the noise of a motorcycle. Heard it stop and start again, and then in the distance the sound of cars and sirens. He was glad he had not been wherever it was. If you were anywhere near that sort of thing you could get mixed up in it. He did not understand that that was precisely what he was already: mixed up in it.

(Jiří stopped speaking. Along the alley on the other side of the garden wall came the soft echo of footsteps. Davie drank his whisky. His eyes were accustomed to the night now. He could see the garden whole, one side bright in the moonlight, the other dark in the shadow of the wall. Since they sat down the shadow had crept across new flowers, and others had emerged into the light. It was like a stage set, Davie was thinking. There were too many flowers, too many English flowers, for Rigoletto's moonlit garden. But that was the sort of thing.

(The footsteps of the night wanderer faded away as they turned into High Street.)

"I was in a busier street now," said Jiří. "There weren't many people about, but I thought each one of them was looking at me, and whispering to each other: 'That's Jiří Vanásek. Where's he going? Watch him.' And in the darkness beyond curtained windows I felt sure there were eyes, watching for me as I came towards them ('Yes—look! Here he comes!') following me into the distance ('Aha! There he goes!') tracking me all the way. But nobody spoke to me, and by the time I had walked past two policemen and several German soldiers, I felt braver. And presently I came in sight of the church.

"I glanced over my shoulder. There was only an old woman. Then I turned down the alley. It didn't seem possible to me that my bicycle could be there—but it was—down at the end—leaning against the wall."

For a few seconds Jiří fell silent. He was thinking of that moment and how he had checked for an instant in his stride.

In the silence Davie stirred in his chair and looked at him.

"Yes?" he said. "Go on."

"I walked down the alley, took my bicycle and wheeled it to the other end. And then, just as I was going to mount it, I heard a voice behind me calling down the alley, 'Hi! You! Where are you going?'

"I would have ridden away without answering but a jeep with soldiers in it was passing the end of the alley. By the time it was out of the way the man was up with me. He was a German policeman.

"'Thieving, eh?' he said.

"'I'm not a thief,' I said. 'This is my bicycle.'

"'What was it doing in the alley?'

"'I left it there.'

"'You left it there? What for?'

"He took me to the police station and brought me in front of two older men. They asked questions, fast and repeatedly. What was my name: where did I live: what did my father do: why was I there: where had I been: where was I going: and since I was young and answered reasonably well they seemed reasonably satisfied.

"'All right, Jiří Vanásek,' said the senior of the three men. 'You can go. But watch out. I've got a note of your name. This isn't the time or the place to be acting strangely. Watch it or you'll be getting into trouble.'

"And then the door opened and a German patrolman came in.

"'Have you heard?' he asked at once. 'There's been big trouble twenty minutes back. Two chaps—'

"And at that moment he saw me.

"'Hallo!' he said. 'What's he done? I've seen that boy once already this afternoon. He was back yonder when the trouble began.'

"'Was he?' said the older man. 'That's interesting. Had he got a bicycle with him?'

"'No. But talking of bicycles, it was on a bicycle one of the chaps got away. Someone saw him. The bicycle was waiting for him. But they lost him. The thing is to find the bicycle. The man won't be far off.'

" 'Yes,' said the senior police officer. 'That's it. Find the bicycle. Maybe we have.'

"You can guess the rest—questions, questions, questions, until I contradicted myself, and then the finding of the man in a cellar near the alley where the bicycle had been. If I'd got there earlier or later it would have been all right. If I'd answered my questions quicker or better I wouldn't have met the patrolman. As it was, I, aged twelve, an enemy of the State, was sent to a concentration camp. My father and mother were sent to another. The owner of the cellar was hanged. The man in the cellar was hanged. I have always felt responsible for four deaths."

"And the man—" began Davie.

"Was Vladimir Kalaš."

"I see."

"Vladimir Kalaš, father of Dalibor, the great violinist."

For several seconds there was silence. Jiři Vanásek had something more to say and he seemed unable to begin. But presently, "Everyone knew my part in the affair," he said "—because of the trial. I had to give evidence. Dalibor was sent to the concentration camp too. He and I had been to school together, and now he met me in a prison."

"Surely he understood?" said Davie.

"In a concentration camp men keep together, try to help each other. But in the year we were there together Dalibor Kalaš only spoke to me once. He said, 'I'll get you, Jiři Vanásek. Somewhere, sometime I'll get you.' "

That was the story that Jiři Vanásek had told to Dr. Davie, sitting in the moonlight by the open door at the back of George's shop. And after waiting silently for half a minute Dr. Davie had said,

"When something appalling happens to one at first one thinks about it all the time, and then gradually one sets it aside and only remembers it irregularly until at last one's sorrow is reduced to a sort of exhibit, like something in a drawer, something one can fish out and look at and say, 'Ah yes—I remember now—that happened to me.' And the old indignation returns, but not to stay. The phrase 'a skeleton in the cupboard' is right—not so much for the word skeleton as for the word cupboard. One takes one's sorrow out from time to time and looks at it, and puts it back again. But one must put it back. That is essential. Thought breaks the heart. Put it away, Jiří."

"I can't. It isn't only a matter of thoughts and memories. There's something else. Eighteen months ago a man called on me. He knew my story. Every detail of it. He indicated that if I wanted it kept quiet I'd better do a little post office work for him. When blackmail doesn't concern oneself one supposes one could laugh it off quite bravely—but when it comes to the point it's not so easy. It seems the best way out, the least trouble. This hasn't cost me money. Only shame and anxiety."

"Can't you get out of it?"

Jiří did not answer at once. He sat quite still, looking at the gate, listening. Presently he said, "Sorry, I thought I heard someone. What did you say?"

"I said, can't you get out of it?"

"I don't know how. Besides, people who quit this sort of job are dangerous liabilities. I think it could be disastrous."

"Who is this man?"

"I don't know. He was of course acting for someone else."

"How often do you get these messages?"

"Irregularly. I got one this morning."

It was characteristic of Davie that he did not ask to see it. If Jiří wanted to show it to him he would do so. Jiří said nothing.

After half a minute's silence Davie said, "The news that you live in King's Lacy would come to these Czechs as a matter of interest. Of course it would. And surely it is reasonable that they should speak of it. But I don't believe revenge lasts that long in a civilized community. As for this other business, I should take it to the police—at once—tomorrow morning."

Wise words, comforting words, Jiří was thinking as he sat in his office, the time nearly midnight. But the fact was that Dr. Davie had heard them talking about him, and Turek had come to the shop, and Dalibor was the son of Vladimir: there was no doubt about that: he had not altered. And besides . . .

A night lorry lumbered down the street, shaking the house. Outside the office door a floor board creaked. And suddenly Jiří felt afraid. As a child fears to go upstairs to bed, so he feared to leave this lighted room, to fumble for the switches, and seek the staircase in the kitchen. He listened. There was no sound at all, except for Eardley Norton telling out the minutes of his life. He was a minute older than he had been a minute ago. He was thirty seconds nearer the grave than he had been when the thought came into his head. The voice of Eardley Norton was the voice of Fate. There was not much to live for, thought Jiří Vanásek. But then he looked up and saw the Meissen Europa, and, yes, he thought, there is.

But he did not get up. He sat very still, as a child might do, unwilling to give a clue to an imaginary listener in the passage.

Presently he found himself looking again at the golden eagle and the circle of glass on his wings. Himself; the table and the bowl of flowers; and the room floating around him; and behind him the door.

And the door was moving.

Jiří gripped the arms of his chair and stared at the glass. It was not an illusion. The door was moving.

He pushed the chair away from him and sprang to his feet.

The door was indeed ajar. But perhaps he hadn't shut it properly. It did ease itself open when the house shook with those damned lorries. He took two steps towards it, grasped the handle and pulled it open.

Then he peered into the passage, dimly illuminated by the light proceeding from the room. There was nobody there.

Across the passage and a little to the right was a curtained recess for hats and coats, umbrellas and bags. Jiří stood absolutely still, staring at the curtain. There could be someone there. For a full half minute he watched it. There was not a shadow of movement. The house was entirely quiet except for Eardley Norton, who sounded more insistent than ever as he marked the passing minutes.

"I'm a bundle of nerves and a fool," said Jiří Vanásek to himself. "This is Sunday morning and a free day. I will take the car down to the sea and spend the whole day in the sun. And so to bed." He put out the light.

X

Ten minutes after Daniel Caske had left the house in Brook Lane Joe Major crossed the bridge, walked up the moonlit path and opened his front door. It was only late at night that he was at home. His days, except Saturdays and Sundays, were spent at Bexminster Electronics, his evenings, all of them, at the King William. It was generally expected by the neighbours that Mr. Major would fall into the brook any night now. But he never did. It was his liver, not his brain, that was hobnailed.

He entered the sitting room and lit a green-shaded lamp on a small table. Then he crossed the room to a Regency alcove at the side of the fireplace and filled his pipe from a tobacco jar. Then he crossed back to the green lamp and lowered himself into a deep leather chair. In the pool of light on the small table by his knee was a glass, a jug, a decanter. Beyond the bright circle faint lights gleamed from distant shelves and tables. These came from the glass paperweights which Joe Major had collected during thirty sentimental years. The room itself was dull and leathery, the room of a pipe-smoking bachelor. But the paperweights were beautiful and marked milestones in his life. The big one, pale blue, pink and white, a little too like cross sections of Edinburgh rock, had been given him by Maria, the Polish girl. She was the one he had loved best. But the paperweight he loved the best was the small, perfectly symmetrical one. A ring of little white circles with a blue center; a ring of blue circles with an orange center; a ring of orange circles with a white center; a ring of green; a ring of blue; a ring of green; a ring of white; and in the center a tiny purple clover leaf. Dear, witty, sensible, amiable Delia had given him that one.

Joe Major was perfectly aware that business colleagues found him slow. It was a queer thing, he used to think—none of those glorious girls had thought him slow. Sometimes in the small hours of the night Joe Major would walk round the room looking at his trophies and wonder how on earth it was that he had never married. Partly it was because most of them had been married to somebody else. And partly? Well, Joe didn't really know: did he tire of them or did they tire of him? Somehow there had always been another till lately. And then he would sit down in his big leather chair again and think he was well out of it, and pour himself out some more whisky, and work until three in the morning. Work was his true love and this was the time when his mind moved best.

It was quiet at night in Brook Lane. If a neighbour went by, late to bed, the steps on the road faded in the distance like sounds defeated. There was no sound properly belonging to Brook Lane but the ripple of water. And so Joe Major lifted his head and listened when he heard footsteps descending the alley. High walls made a sharp little echo. Then a crunch on the road, and a click at the gate. Someone was walking up the garden path.

Joe Major got up and peered out of the open window.

"I knew you'd be up, you old devil."

William Carroll was standing on the path.

"What are you up to?" said Joe Major from the window.

"I was at Lacy for the concert and stayed on for a drink—and then Philip asked me to help bring the Quartet back. A cello takes up the whole of the back seat. So he took three and I took one, and I've just deposited mine at the Baggot. Then, as I was feeling very awake, I thought I'd call. It's early for you."

"It is. Come on in."

Carroll opened the front door, took three strides along the passage, turned the handle on the left, and entered the dimly lighted room.

"Was it a success—the concert I mean?" It could only be a question of politeness. Joe Major, as Daniel Caske had proclaimed, was wonderfully allergic to music.

"Very much so."

"Half a minute while I get you a glass." Joe ambled out of the room, continuing his conversation as he went. "And the party?" he shouted from the kitchen.

"Just the family. The Czechs didn't want to stop long. Especially as they hadn't very much English between the lot of them. So we were away soon after eleven."

"And then I suppose," said Joe Major, returning, "you started drinking with them at the Baggot."

"I did not."

"You've taken the hell of a time getting here then," said Joe Major, pouring whisky.

"There were all the gracious goodbyes, but it's—what is it?" He looked at his watch. "It's only just gone half past eleven."

Joe Major looked at the clock on the mantelshelf.

"So it is. Sit down."

The little table with the green-shaded lamp stood between them. From the depths of their chairs each saw the other sunk in shadows.

"Joe."

"William."

"You remember last October."

"I do."

"Who did it?"

"You mean—"

"You know what I mean, Joe. There was a leak."

"You don't think it was coincidence?"

"Not a coincidence, Joe. A leak. No one ever produced any evidence of a leak. But it was a leak."

For half a minute Joe Major lay quite still, looking down at his glass balanced in both hands on his broad middle. Then, "There's a sort of leak that's impossible to stop, if it's there," he said. "Things stored in the head aren't subject to security checks."

"Precisely."

Joe looked across the table to the shadowed figure of his

visitor sprawled in the deep chair. The word had sounded loaded.

"Are you hinting at anything, William?"

"No. It's come into my head because we've just had a meeting. I keep wondering if Alec Rowan has really taken any steps about it."

"I would think so, William. Alec's deep."

"Deep as hell. I just get the feeling somebody doesn't want to find out. Those Japs are very efficient. We know that. But twice now they've come to conclusions a bit too quickly. I don't believe it's accidental."

"As of now, William," said Joe Major, falling into his official jargon, "you don't know a damned thing."

"No. I don't."

"Well, if that's settled, have another drink."

"No—I won't, thanks. I only thought I'd look in as I was practically on the doorstep. It's ten minutes to twelve. Home."

"Goodnight. I'm glad you came in, William."

On Joe Major's little bridge Carroll paused and listened to the brook. Joe had planted kingcups and forget-me-nots there. He could see them swaying gently as moonlit leaves touched the water.

A few minutes later he was driving down empty High Street, its ancient houses mysteriously shadowed like an illustration to a ghost story, and prinking towards him on the left hand pavement, like some midnight hag on her unlawful occasions, Mrs. Bazeley. She had been sitting up late doing sums. The night air had invited her, and she had accepted, and there she was, padding along the street towards George's shop, puce cheekbones on a field of beige, hideously topped with a pale mauve scarf. In the brief moment of passing she seemed to William Carroll like an emissary of the Angel of Death.

The next minute he was out on the open road, heading for Combe Magna. It had been a long day, from roses to music and mystery. And it was not quite finished. As he opened his front door the telephone started to ring.

"I hoped I'd catch you," said the voice of Joe Major. "Did you know you'd dropped your ring?"

"I did not. Gosh! I'd have been worried as hell. Where was it?"

"On the carpet by your chair."

"I knew it was a bit loose. I wouldn't have lost it for a wilderness of monkeys. Thanks, Joe."

"Not a bit. Goodnight again."

"Goodnight."

Joe rang off, and "Gosh!" said William Carroll, surveying his little finger. "That was lucky."

XI

Sitting in her bedroom in the house in Abbey Street, Bexminster, Amy Caske heard the front door open and shut. She looked at the watch on her wrist. It was twenty past twelve. She felt certain that Daniel had left the golf club dinner at about ten. She had been at a grass widow's bridge party at Maureen Rowan's in Philpot Way. Alec Rowan had got home at half past ten.

"Just to say goodnight, ladies," he had said, poking his head round the drawing room door. "Good, and I trust honest, playing by one and all. I'm off to bed."

"Alec!"

But it was no good Maureen saying that. Alec did not enjoy being odd man out at a hen party.

So—Alec had come in at half past ten, and it had taken Daniel two and a half hours to drive from King's Lacy.

Amy had a reason for being upset. That evening on her way home from the Guild meeting Mrs. Cowd had dropped in for a chat. And presently, "You know, Amy, I am not one to gossip," she had said, and then had hinted things about Daniel, that Amy "ought to know, if only to refute them," things Amy had never suspected, things that she couldn't believe. Normally Amy would have been asleep an hour ago, wouldn't have known when Daniel came in: but tonight she had waited anxiously—and it was twenty past twelve.

She knew it would anger him, but she could not help it. She opened her door and went to the head of the stairs.

"Daniel!"

"Yes," said Daniel from the kitchen.

"Do you know the time?"

"Of course I do."

"Where have you been?"

Daniel came out of the kitchen, and she saw how grey and tired he looked.

"The car broke down," he said. "I've had to walk most of the way from King's Lacy."

"Five miles in two and a half hours is not very good going," said Amy. And then, because she couldn't think of anything else to say which would not open some irreparable breach, she turned about abruptly and went back to her room.

"But his face—Daniel's face!" she was saying to herself. "He's tired out. I don't believe that Cowd woman."

Almost she decided to go back, to make it up with him, to get him a hot drink—something, anything. But then she heard Daniel's heavy step on the stairs and presently the snap of his bedroom door.

If there had been a chance there, Amy had lost it.

XII

Lying in her bed at Morton Lodge, Bexminster, Mrs. Coppleston heard the clock in the hall strike two. She must have fallen asleep and Robert had not come to her door as she had so often asked him to do.

Two o'clock! Mrs. Coppleston sat up in bed, put on her bedside lamp and listened. There was nothing to hear except the rapid fussy tick-tock-tick-tock of the small clock on the dressing table. Just as though it had something to tell me, thought Mrs. Coppleston with a gay little smile, for (as she frequently told her friends) she could always see the funny side of things.

She got out of bed, put on her dressing gown, opened her door, and walked to the head of the stairs. The light was still on in the hall. Surely if Robert had returned he would have put it out. Pursing her lips and drawing her eyebrows together in a long-practiced expression of maternal anxiety, Mrs. Coppleston crossed the landing and opened Robert's door.

"Robert! Are you there, dear? I have been so worried. I wish you would always come to my door when you come in late."

And then, as Robert did not answer, she moved softly towards the bed and laid her hand on the pillow.

The bed was empty.

At three o'clock Mrs. Coppleston telephoned to the police. And the Bexminster police, because of her importunity, telephoned the King's Lacy police, much to the annoyance of Sergeant Clegg, who was in a ripe slumber, and quite unable, at that hour of night, to cope with such vague information.

Sunday

I

At half past twelve on Sunday morning William Carroll left the rose garden and returned to the house to tidy up for lunch. From time to time, while struggling with the Albertine rose, he had considered the mystery of the previous afternoon. He had told Philip Gossamer that he would telephone Coppleston in the morning. He had not yet done so, but he supposed he had better get it over. He stopped in the hall and dialled the number.

It was answered almost as soon as it began to ring.

"Mrs. Coppleston speaking. Is that Sergeant—"

"This is William Carroll, Mrs. Coppleston."

"Oh."

The voice sounded disappointed.

"Is Robert in?"

"No, Mr. Carroll, he is not, and I am terribly worried about him. He did not return last night. He set off for Roughton at about noon, and simply disappeared. He said he was going to Witherby in the afternoon, and then in the evening to the concert at Lacy. Whether he was at the concert I don't know, but he didn't go to Merry's at Roughton. Just in case he'd altered his plans I rang up Mrs. Bazeley in King's Lacy. He often goes there—but she says she hasn't seen him. I've told the police—that's why I thought it might be them calling. I'm terribly, terribly worried."

"I can throw a little light on this, Mrs. Coppleston—though nothing good I'm afraid. Your son telephoned to me from the King William at about half past one. He asked if he could come to see me on business."

"Yes?"

"But he never arrived."

"Please, Mr. Carroll—ring the police station and tell them this. It will give them some direction. They have no idea where to start looking. If Robert has had an accident it must have been somewhere between King's Lacy and Combe Magna. He might have been knocked down by a car and left in a ditch. Please, please, do something quickly."

"I'll ring the police at once. One other thing. I don't think Robert was at the concert. I was there. I didn't see him. I'm terribly sorry."

"Thank you. Thank you so much. I won't keep you talking."

Then William Carroll rang the police station, and told them about yesterday's telephone call. "As Coppleston was speaking from the King William," he added, "there may be someone there who saw him or spoke to him. There would surely be regulars who might have noticed him."

It was not so surely. The majority of lunchers at the King William had been visitors. Robert Coppleston meant nothing to them. But there were two people who could tell a little. Alec Rowan and Daniel Caske both told the police that they had seen Robert Coppleston enter George's. They had not seen him come out.

Then—it was past four o'clock by now—the police had telephoned Jiří Vanásek. There was no answer. That was not surprising. Mr. Vanásek was usually away on a Sunday. Still, if Coppleston had last been seen entering George's they would have to find Mr. Vanásek. So Sergeant Clegg laboriously concluded. And then P. C. Whimple tapped on his door and asked if he would see a Dr. Davie.

"I think he knows something about Robert Coppleston, Sergeant."

Davie had come round because he had heard about the inquiries from Alice.

"There won't have been many people here that knew Mr. Coppleston," Alice had said. "He lived over at Bexminster, and he didn't come in here very often. And nearly all our people at lunch time were Festival visitors—naturally. Mr. Rowan and Mr. Caske knew him, of course—they're to do with Bexminster Electrics or whatever the name is. They always lunch here of a Saturday before playing golf. Mr. Major would have known him too. He was here yesterday. Only he spends all his time in the bar . . . Mr. Major likes veal and ham pie," said Alice, as though she were offering a rational explanation for his absences from the dining room.

And so at five o'clock on Sunday afternoon Davie called at the King's Lacy police station and was ushered into the presence of Sergeant Clegg.

"Dr. Davie, Sergeant," said P.C. Whimple.

"Good evening."

The Sergeant indicated a chair.

"Please sit down. I understand you have something to tell me about Robert Coppleston."

"Yes. It was only this: I am staying at the King William: I

was lunching in the window yesterday, and I happened to see a young man parking his bicycle by George's, and then entering the shop. I wouldn't have known who he was if my neighbours had not seen him too, and mentioned his name."

"Do you know who they were?"

"A Mr. Rowan and a Mr. Caske."

The Sergeant nodded. Nothing new so far.

"About twenty minutes later I was in the hall of the King William as someone in the telephone box was finishing a conversation. I heard this person say to a Mr. Carroll that he didn't want to take something or other to Mr. Rowan or Sir Philip—Sir Philip Gossamer, I suppose—and that he would come along at once to see Mr. Carroll. And then he left the hotel. I was going out for a walk at the same time and I saw him collect his bicycle and set off down the street. It was only then that I realized it was the same young man that I had seen entering George's. That's all. Not very much, I'm afraid."

"Mr. Carroll has already told me about the telephone call."

"Ah."

"But we hadn't found anyone who saw him actually start. We are a little further forward."

"About a hundred yards," said Davie. "I last saw him passing the traffic lights in the middle of High Street."

"You didn't know what this was that he wanted to take to Mr. Carroll?"

"I've no idea at all."

Neither has Mr. Carroll, the Sergeant was thinking. And neither, obviously, has Mr. Rowan or Sir Philip Gossamer.

"Of course," said Davie quietly, " 'it' may not have been anything tangible. He might have meant he didn't want to take some story or problem to the other two."

"H'm," said Sergeant Clegg. That was not what he had gathered from Mr. Carroll. "Well—thank you Dr. Davie for calling. Should we want you again you are at the King William?"

"Yes, for a few days. I'm here for the Festival."

And so Davie made his way back to the King William to change and have an early dinner, and then at a quarter past seven to make his way up High Street to the Corn Exchange. It was the first night of the opera—the Sunday performance limited to members of the Festival Club, that devious arrangement for escaping the regulations, smacking so pleasantly of the eighteenth century.

II

The search for Robert Coppleston had gone on all Sunday afternoon, and there was no one among the searchers who did not feel at the back of his mind that he was engaged on a futile operation. Robert Coppleston was not a child. The country bordering the road between King's Lacy and Combe Magna was not a pathless forest. It was open farming country and it held no secrets. There were ditches beside the road, but there was not the slightest difficulty in investigating them. From the crossroads in King's Lacy High Street to the gates of Combe Court they had searched every yard of the way. There was not a sign of Robert Coppleston or of his bicycle. Nor in this fine dry weather was there any track of a wheel in the drive. Nor was there anyone living in houses by the road who was prepared to say that he had seen a cyclist resembling Robert Coppleston. If he had indeed ridden along that road there must have been many motorists who had passed him, but where were they now? They might be in Scotland by this time. The plain fact was that at present there was no proof at all that Robert Coppleston had ever turned down that side road with the crazy signpost, the road to Combe Magna.

He was not a child, the searchers repeated. The probability was that he was not within miles of Combe Magna.

At eight o'clock the search was called off.

Meanwhile, at half past seven, with nothing to distract from the occasion, the curtain had risen on the Festival Club's special performance of the principal event of the week.

Anatole Bysshe had spent six months searching for a work that no one had ever seen and few had ever heard of, and had finally settled on *The Fairies*. Not of course Wagner's first effort, *Die Feen:* that would have been far too simple. Besides, it was a hundred years too late. There would have been no fun restoring it. No, *The Fairies*, uncovered, restored, re-orchestrated, "realized" by Anatole Bysshe, was a piece arranged for Drury Lane in 1755 from *A Midsummer Night's Dream*, "the songs from Shakespeare, Milton, Waller, Dryden, Hammond, &c.," a remarkable work in which Puck sings "Where the bee sucks," Oberon "Sigh no more, Ladies," and Titania "Orpheus with his lute"—while Helena, at the end of the piece, remarks

> Storms and tempests may blow over,
>   And subside to gentle gales,
> So the poor despairing lover,
>   When least hoping, oft prevails—

which was possibly contributed by &c.

This entertaining literary curiosity had long held an honoured place in Davie's library, for the first edition is the only edition, and he had been fortunate enough to find it bound up with a number of other eighteenth century operas. For the libretto's sake alone he would have hastened to any production.

But there was a second and a juster reason for welcoming *The Fairies*—the reason (to be fair) which had engaged Anatole Bysshe's loving attention in the first place. The music was by the almost forgotten John Christopher Smith, pupil and amanuensis of Handel, composer of some delightful music for the harpsichord and of the opera *Ulysses* (1733), a splendid work revived at the St. Pancras Festival of 1965. J. C. Smith was a fine rediscovery and Anatole Bysshe and Mrs. Manifold had decidedly "done it again."

In the original production Oberon had been played by Master Reinholt and Puck by Master Moore, deadly words suggesting performances by infant phenomenons, that tedious infirmity of the eighteenth- and early nineteenth-century theater.° Mrs. Manifold's Oberon and Puck were splendid young men with excellent voices, though it was wickedly suggested that their costumes were the principal reason for the immediate sale on Monday morning of all remaining tickets for later performances. In other ways, too, the thing had been most rewarding to the eye, and it was admirably sung by everyone. The curtain had fallen on a storm of applause and Mrs. Manifold had received a curtain call and a whopping great bouquet—though she would of course have received both in any event.

As the audience spilled out onto the pavement everyone was contributing something to that excited rumble which indicated success.

"I don't care if it *is* derivative—it was gorgeous."

"My dear! Those costumes!"

° At almost exactly the same date the part of Tom Thumb was being played at Norwich by Master Hinde, aged five.

"It was terribly funny and absolutely delicious at the same time."

And dominating her immediate vicinity, Mrs. Mapleton-Morley:

"Have you got everything, Janet? You usually manage to leave something."

"Everything, Aunt Maud," said Miss Bangle, "except a foolish heart that I leave here behind."

"What are you talking about, Janet?"

"It's what Helena says in the play—only of course it wasn't in this version. What I mean is that I think George Commice is wonderful as Oberon."

"H'm," said Mrs. Mapleton-Morley, "I hope he won't catch cold. I preferred the two lovers."

An eddy in the flow of scarves and wraps and bodies brought Lady Meade-Fuller within hailing distance of Davie.

"Wasn't it splendid, R.V.?"

"Splendid indeed; Three cheers for Mrs. Manifold. I particularly liked the rabbits."

"And three cheers for Smith, too, R.V."

"Certainly. Just for tonight Smith is my favourite composer."

Waving a despairing hand Mildred Meade-Fuller suddenly disappeared, engulfed in a counter-current of friends. And "I do so agree, Dr. Davie," said the voice of Mrs. Mapleton-Morley. "Do join us for a drink at the King William, won't you?"

"I—er—" There really was no escape. "Thank you—thank you," said Davie. "I shall be delighted."

Head above the crowd, Richard Serpent flowed, cheerful and relaxed. He had seen the recent production of *Ulysses* and he had written about that in the notice he had already composed about *The Fairies*. It only remained to add a bit about the singing and the costumes, and to dredge up some entertaining adjectives. It would be jolly amusing to say the fairies were a bit camp. He hadn't used "camp" for several weeks—not since his sauce-box notice of *Idomeneo*. It would be just right. Richard Serpent surveyed the crowd with a complacent smile. He had a pleasant evening ahead of him.

Little Pincock was looking less at ease. He was at a sad loss for something to dispute. He would doubtless think of something. At any rate the problem enabled him to say, "No thank you, Mrs. Mapleton-Morley, but I can't really. I have to write my wretched review."

They walked on towards the King William.

"It was nice and short," said Mrs. Mapleton-Morley with a fat sigh. "Everything nowadays is too long."

"I don't know about 'nowadays,'" said Davie. "I have always thought the masters should have been more careful with their masterpieces. There's hardly one that wouldn't have been better for shortening. Once the composer is dead it becomes a sacrilege to touch it—but if only, in the making, the maestro had paused to consider the customers, to reckon the limits of human endurance!"

"I hope you're not going to say—" began Miss Bangle.

"Not I!" said Davie. "I name no names."

"I'm so glad."

"I merely remark that Genius claims peculiar privileges in the field of boredom."

Still with the crowd emerging from the Corn Exchange, William Carroll steered Sir Philip Gossamer into the shadow of an early Victorian statesman on a plinth—in fact Sir Philip's great-grandfather, petrified, so it appeared, in the act of commending, or possibly condemning, the Corn Laws.

"Did you hear about Coppleston?" he asked.

"No. Was it all right?"

"It wasn't."

"Really?"

"He hasn't turned up. He didn't go home. He's disappeared."

"That's odd. There must be a reason. Felt like a weekend away from Mamma, I expect."

"But why telephone me and say he was coming?"

"That's strange, I agree."

"Mrs. Coppleston's told the police and they've been looking for him."

A look of urbane annoyance occupied Philip Gossamer's face for a moment.

"I hope there isn't going to be a lot of publicity."

"Bound to be some."

"Well—do let me know if you hear anything. Excuse me, William. I've got to go round behind to see Mrs. Manifold and Bysshe and all the rest of it. It was a great success, I think."

" 'There must be a reason,' " muttered Carroll to himself. "Of course there must. That's the point."

He made his way round to the car park. Philip's eternal poise, he was thinking—it must be put on. He can't be indifferent to everything except his social obligations. He does it all so well. But he's so cold. He's an image. You can't stir him. You can't tell what he's thinking about.

Out of the bonnet of a car a bent figure straightened and waved an imploring arm.

"Oh—Mr. Carroll! Would you be very kind and do me a service?"

It was old Dew, a Combe Magna neighbour.

"With pleasure. What's the trouble?"

"My car won't start. I never did understand the inside of a

car. I've pressed all the various buttons and nothing happens at all."

Carroll investigated.

"You haven't got any petrol in the tank."

"No *petrol*! What an extraordinary thing! What can I do now?"

"You better hop into my car, and come back in the morning."

"May I? That would be kind. Really most kind."

"Not a bit."

"I can't think how I could have been so careless."

"It's happened to all of us. Jump in. Is your door shut?"

Three minutes later they were speeding along the road towards the golf links.

"Goodness!" said Mr. Dew. He was not accustomed to riding in a Jaguar.

Eyes glittering in the car lights, a rabbit bundled across the road. Carroll slowed down abruptly. He had a peculiar horror of those little patches of blood-stained fur left on the highroad for the sun to find, bunny or more often the slow hedgehog, not just killed, but flattened.

"Well done!" said Mr. Dew, secretly grateful to the rabbit.

Then the signpost to Combe Magna grew in the lights, and the car turned smoothly down the lane. Here were higher hedges and overhanging trees and wild flowers that had escaped the poisonous attentions of the farmers—campion, stitchwort, speedwell, meadowsweet, ferns, all momentarily stereoscopic and sharp against the shadows.

"It's beautiful at night, our hill," said Mr. Dew.

Halfway down Combe Hill, on the right, under the branches of a mighty beech, the white gates of Combe Court gleamed in the car lights.

"Come up to the house for a drink?" asked Carrroll.

"Oh no—thank you very much. It's too late. I'll get out at the gate. It's only a few yards."

"Just let me turn into the drive."

It was an awkward turn and it had to be taken gracefully. As the slowly circling lamps swept the rhododendron hedge each dark leaf shone in the surrounding shadow. And suddenly between the branches a glittering light replied like a signal.

"I wonder what that is," said Mr. Dew.

"What was it?" said Carroll, intent on completing the turn.

"That light—in the hedge—it's gone now."

Carroll stopped the car inside the drive and got out with Mr. Dew.

"What light?" he said. "Show me."

They walked back to the road.

"It's not there now," said Mr. Dew. "It must have been a reflection of the car lights."

"Yes—but from what?"

They moved down the road a little, and there where the moon shone on the hedge, "Look!" said Mr. Dew. "There it is."

It came from behind the hedge—a small point of light, bright as silver is bright, as mercury is bright.

"What do you think it is?" asked Mr. Dew.

Carroll returned to the car and groped for a torch. Then, making himself a path between two rhododendrons, he worked his way into the bushes and back towards the road. Nervously behind him stepped Mr. Dew.

Almost at once, between the branches, the torch awoke an answering light, and Carroll, stepping between two great bushes, reached a small open space and found what he was looking for.

Handlebars.

"Oh dear!" whispered Mr. Dew in the darkness. "This is terrible. What shall we do, Mr. Carroll, what shall we do?"

Robert Coppleston had got to Combe Court after all. But he lay there with a great bruise on the side of his neck, the contents of his pockets scattered on the earth.

Monday

I

ON MONDAY MORNING MRS. BAZELEY WAS AWAKE AT SIX-thirty. She usually woke early, but this morning she was feeling particularly spry, having spent the whole of Sunday morning in bed, reading the newspapers, planning and dozing, the three all muddled up together between cigarettes and cups of overdrawn tea. From time to time Mrs. Bazeley's familiar, a tabby called Tommy, would walk gingerly up the bed and push a bulge in Mrs. Bazeley's newspaper, or peer round the edge at her, and, if she still took no notice of him, would advance to the pillow and pat her gently on the face with a velvet paw, an engaging trick which betrayed even the flinty heart of Mrs. Bazeley. Then she would lay down the paper and pour Tommy out a saucer of milk, and when he had licked it dry and had retired to the bottom of the bed, she would pour herself out another poisoned chalice, and return to the papers.

At nine o'clock the telephone rang. She thought of not answering it, changed her mind and regretted it. Mr. Coppleston's mother? What a nuisance!

"Yes," said Mrs. Bazeley. "Yes, I know Mr. Coppleston. What's the matter with him? . . . No . . . He often does come here. But he didn't come yesterday . . . Quite certain . . . No . . . I know nothing about him at all . . . Sorry I can't help you . . . Goodbye."

"God! What a carry-on!" Mrs. Bazeley added, almost before she had cradled the telephone.

She retrieved the pages of her untidy paper. Except for the political part, which she considered a bore, and where the hell was North Korea anyway, Mrs. Bazeley read the lot—take-over bids, scandal at the barracks, holiday islands ripe for development, boxing, gardening, cooking, bridge: she even bothered to place in order of merit six equally hideous lady's frocks. And then there were the auction articles—the furniture, the porcelain, the jewellery. £5,000 for that tiara! £5,000, thought Mrs. Bazeley, lowering the paper and bending her eye on vacancy. £5,000!

The newsprint faded from her mind as a transparency in the theater fades. In its place Mrs. Bazeley saw the bits of jewellery on the green velvet in the window downstairs. She began to make familiar calculations. She had sold two bits to that American woman on Saturday. If she could sell them all at those prices she reckoned she would make a profit of £176 10s. Which was not bad.

The jewellery and the green velvet fading in turn, Mrs. Bazeley found herself staring across the bedroom at the two new Staffordshire figures—a young man and a sheep and a young woman and a sheep, each beneath a spreading tree of white, laced with deliciously improbable gold squiggles. A splendid pair, but ill at ease on that dressing table surrounded with powder puffs and sticks of Mrs. Bazeley's remarkable makeup. Mr. Coppleston would certainly buy them. But Mr. Coppleston knew what was what. She wouldn't get any fancy prices out of him.

And that brought her to the Chippendale armchair. She meant to have that chair. It went against her grain to speculate on what might prove to be a powerful old age, but the only certain way, it seemed to her, was to buy it *now*, cash down for £5—well £8 if necessary—on the understanding that the old girl should keep it during her lifetime. And please God that might not be too long to wait. Of course it would all have to be written down. She might have to pay £10. Not a penny more.

Not a penny more, thought Mrs. Bazeley, lifting the paper again. And so that vision faded and her eyes took in the newsprint again, and presently she was absorbed in "recent wills." £30,000—Miss Tozer: £54,000—Miss Gander: £82,-000—Sir George Puker. Goodness! Mrs. Bazeley was the last person to favour a fair distribution of wealth. But it was provoking reading. And then, speculating happily on what she would do in the unlikely event of being left a huge fortune, Mrs. Bazeley fell into a delicious doze, from which she was awakened by Tommy, who, dismayed at being still without a proper breakfast at lunch time, advanced up the bed, patted Mrs. Bazeley on the face, bent down his head and purred loudly in her ear.

"Go away, Tommy," said Mrs. Bazeley.

Tommy went away. He jumped off the bed, jumped onto the dressing table, and from there ascended the mantelshelf. Then, delicately stepping across various objects of assorted *vertu*, Tommy poised himself on the end of the shelf and deliberately took a flying leap onto the bed again.

"Tommy!"

Mrs. Bazeley was out of bed in a flash. It was a maneuver that never failed.

"You fiend!" said Mrs. Bazeley, but not crossly. She admired Tommy's ruthless sagacity, and anyway it was past one o'clock.

So Mrs. Bazeley put on a housecoat covered with pink roses and eagerly preceded by Tommy, who appeared to fear that his mistress might be in some doubt as to the whereabouts of the larder, went downstairs and produced cold salmon for both of them and strawberries and cream; for Mrs. Bazeley was no miser in matters which concerned her comfort. If she had ever asked anyone to lunch that person would have been well served.

The afternoon was spent by both of them in the garden, dozing in the sunshine.

At half past six Mrs. Bazeley heard the music of evensong floating down the street from the church of St. Stephen. And suddenly it made her feel very serious and religious and reminiscent of church-goings years ago with her mother and brother, Sam. Poor Sam, poor Sam. Killed in that awful war. Then she found herself thinking of old Mr. Snow, who used to sit behind them, and sang every word of the psalms at the top of his voice. "For his mercy endureth forever"; twenty-six times repeated, and Mr. Snow never missed one of them. And then there was Miss Troak, who marshalled the infants to church and used her umbrella to discipline distant offenders, rewarding inattention with pokes in the back and even smart blows on the head, to the great delight of neighbouring worshippers.

Mrs. Bazeley admitted to herself that she ought to go to church more often. It was too late this evening, but next week, she thought as she heaved herself out of her deck chair, next week perhaps. "For his mercy endureth forever," sang Mrs. Bazeley to herself. She could hear the voice of old Snow singing it. Then she went into the kitchen and mixed herself a large gin and tonic and brought it back to the garden together with a saucer of milk for Tommy, who was engaged in stalking a wasp.

Yes, what with one indulgence and another, Sunday had been a restful day and Mrs. Bazeley was back in bed again by nine o'clock, listening to Your Hundred Best Tunes; and soon, wondering vaguely how some of the tunes could ever have been anybody's best, she fell asleep and did not wake again till half past six on Monday morning.

And that was why she and Tommy were up so early, and why at half past eight she was standing at the shop door, surveying the sunny street, and meditating a call on Jiří Vanásek. There wasn't much Mrs. B didn't know about who had bought what, and where, and for how much. She wanted very much to see the Europa—and the best way of doing that, she thought, was to pay a friendly call while ostensibly engaged on the morning's shopping. On the pavement she hesitated. Then, returning to the shop, she fished one of the Bristol cups out of the window, wrapped it up carefully in a sheet of wadding and popped it into her capacious shopping bag. She would ask Jiří's opinion about it. That would be an excellent opening.

As she set off along the almost empty High Street the hands of St. Stephen's clock stood at twenty minutes to nine.

II

"There's nothing else you can tell us, sir?" said Detective Inspector Tabor of the County Constabulary. Tabor had been summoned at an early hour by Sergeant Clegg of the King's Lacy Police. He was now going over the ground from the beginning and, after the evidence of Mr. Carroll, the beginning seemed to him to spring from the last man who had seen Robert Coppleston alive—or was so far supposed to have been the last to see him alive.

"There's nothing else you can tell us, sir?"

Davie considered the question for a few seconds. He was sensitive about being taken for some fictional know-all. Eventually he said, "There is one thing, one small thing. When I came out of the dining room there was no one in the hall, but I did notice that the door into the lounge was in the process of closing itself—which meant that someone had just used it. If someone had come *out* of the lounge I would have seen him—so I presume that someone had just gone *into* the lounge."

"You mean—"

"I mean that someone else had just been in the hall and could have overheard some earlier part of the telephone conversation."

Inspector Tabor stared at Dr. R. V. Davie. Was this brilliantly perceptive, or faintly absurd? His first reaction was against percipience, but after tilting his chair back and tapping the end of his nose several times with the end of a pencil, he said, "Do you know who was in the lounge at the time, sir?"

"Several people were drinking coffee after lunch. I don't know who they were except for Mr. Rowan and Mr. Caske. I'd sat next to them at lunch. I saw them through the glass door. There was a third man talking to them. They were sitting. He was standing, leaning over Mr. Rowan's chair and talking rather eagerly."

"There will be no difficulty in checking on that."

"And I think we already know," said Sergeant Clegg, consulting his notes of the previous day. "I think it was Mr. Major, another of the Bexminster directors."

"He was a middle-aged chap with a good head of fair hair and a decidedly rubicund face," said Davie.

"Mr. Major," said Clegg.

"It was just a thought," said Davie.

Tabor said nothing—except "Come in" to a knocker at the door.

P. C. Whimple entered with a tray and laid it on the inspector's table.

"The things that were lying by the body, sir."

"Right."

"And this bit of paper, sir. There was a hole in his coat pocket. This was inside the lining."

Tabor took the paper, looked at it, turned it over, and pursed his lips. "All right," he said, and the constable left the room.

Tabor laid the paper down on the table. It hardly seemed to have aroused his interest. To Davie the marks were upside down, but reading things upside down had always entertained him: he had no difficulty in deciphering these.

"Will you excuse me if I butt in," he said. "It's not my business—but I think I've seen that before."

"What? This paper?"

"Yes."

"You have? Where?"

"In George's shop—the antique shop. It was inside a lidded sugar bowl. I noticed it because I thought it was odd. It wasn't a price, or even a code of a price."

Tabor considered. "It's a very ordinary bit of paper. Why should it be the same?"

"I think it is," said Davie.

Again Inspector Tabor stared very hard at Dr. R. V. Davie.

"Have you any idea what it means?"

"None at all. But—if I am right—it seems to have been sufficiently interesting for Mr. Coppleston to have taken it away."

Again Tabor tilted his chair back and tapped his nose rhythmically with his pencil. Then, "Yes," he said. "I see what you mean. It could be important."

He brought his chair down again with decision.

"We can very soon settle that by calling on Mr. Vanásek. I'll be obliged if you'll come with me, sir."

"Now?"

"Yes, sir, right away. I've got a car."

III

"We can go to the shop door," Tabor had said. "He'll be open by this time." But the door had been shut, and they had walked down the alley and rung the bell at Mr. Vanásek's back door. There was no answer.

Then Tabor tried the handle and the door opened.

"He's up," said Tabor.

"Jiří! Are you in?" called Davie.

For a few seconds they waited. Then, "Where was this paper?" asked Tabor.

"In the shop—in a gold and white tea service—shall I look? Or ought we to wait for him?"

"Look. No harm in that. You were looking before."

So they passed through the kitchen and into the shop. And Davie went to the Worcester tea service, lifted the lid of the sugar bowl, peered inside, and put the lid back again.

"It's gone," he said.

"Gone, has it? Now that is a bit odd. Where is he? Why doesn't he come?"

Davie moved back to the kitchen and called up the stairs. "Jiří! Mr. Vanásek! Are you there?"

There was no answer.

"He certainly isn't in."

"The front door locked and the back door open," said Tabor. "That's careless."

He walked through the shop.

"What's in here?"

"That's the office."

Tabor opened the door. The office had no windows and when the light was off the room was but dimly illuminated by the outside day. Davie, who was standing immediately behind him, could see nothing but the policeman's back. But he sensed that Tabor suddenly stood rigidly still. Then, without speaking, he put out a hand and touched the electric switch.

"Don't come in, Dr. Davie," he said. "And don't touch anything, sir—particularly not that door."

Then, very cautiously, he moved into the room and knelt down beside the man who lay face downwards on the floor.

"Can you say if it's Vanásek?" Tabor asked.

"Yes," said Davie from the doorway. "I'm sure it is. I remember that suit."

Tabor leaned over the body and peered at the man's face. "It's exactly the same as the other," he said softly. "That blow on the throat."

Tabor got up, and for a minute stood there, not speaking, looking around him. Then, "The door was open, but it wasn't forced, and the shop isn't disturbed. Here's a man dead, but it doesn't look as though he's been robbed. The safe isn't bust. One can't tell if anything's missing, but it doesn't look like it."

Immediately in Davie's line of sight from the door was the

cabinet and above it the golden eagle and the convex looking glass.

"I would think there is one thing missing, Inspector," he said. "A porcelain group known as the Meissen Europa. It was there on the cabinet on Saturday night at half past eleven. It's not there now."

Back at the police station twenty minutes later Davie said, "I think I might well have been the last person to see Mr. Vanásek alive. You see I gave him a lift home from the concert, he asked me in for a drink, and I stayed talking with him till half past eleven. Mr. Vanásek let me out at the front door and I went straight across to the hotel."

"Was the porter on duty?"

"Yes, he was. I've no doubt he'll remember."

"You were sitting with Mr. Vanásek for an hour?"

"Yes."

"Where were you, sir?"

"Outside the kitchen door at the back of the house. It was a moonlight night and very warm, you remember. We had no light—didn't need any. We had taken our chairs to the little terrace overlooking the garden."

"When you left, sir, Mr. Vanásek would have had to un-lock the front door to let you out?"

"Yes."

"Did he lock it again?"

"That I don't know. He stood at the open door, watching me till I entered the hotel. But surely he would have done so."

After a pause the policeman said, "Did he lock the back door when you left your places by the door?"

"No, he didn't. I'm sure about that. We got up and walked straight into the shop."

"It's open now. How long do you think, sir, it might have been before he could have got back to that door?"

"We stopped a few seconds at the office door, we walked across the shop, and exchanged a few farewell remarks, and then he stayed at the door and watched me cross the road. Say, twenty, thirty, thirty-five, fifty, sixty seconds—locking the front door, sixty-five seconds, and back to the kitchen—seventy-five seconds. A minute and a quarter at least: but, of course, if he did anything on the way back . . ."

"The point is that the place hasn't been broken into. Therefore—either, after you'd gone, Mr. Vanásek intentionally let in whoever it was that attacked him, or that person got into the house through the back door while he was absent at the front. The door has bolts, not a lock. If the murderer went out at the back he wouldn't have been able to fix the door—and that's probably the reason why it's open."

"I'm not so sure of that," said Davie. "It's better to come out boldly from a front door than to risk being seen sneaking out of a back door. And I notice that the front door isn't double locked: it's only on the Yale—which suggests a door pulled to from outside. The man might have thought the back door *was* bolted. He might have known it wasn't, and still have preferred to use the front door. Or he might not have thought about it at all. Murderers can't afford to waste time."

"H'm," said Tabor. "There's one other question, Dr. Davie."

"Yes?"

He knew what it was going to be, and he didn't know how to answer it. He didn't want to give Jiří's confidences away. He didn't want to throw suspicion on those Czechs without better evidence than Jiří's fears.

107

"Have you any reason to suppose that Mr. Vanásek feared an attack might be made on him?"

There it was.

"He was in a very nervy and depressed state, certainly. And the reason was that he had been to the concert at Lacy to hear the Czech quartet. It reminded him of his experiences as a boy and the terrors of the German occupation twenty-five years back. I'd overheard one of the players mention his name and I told him, thinking it would interest him. But it didn't; it upset him; upset him to think that people out there still remembered him, and perhaps resented his having changed his country."

"Resented his behaviour enough to do—this?" said Tabor, raising his eyebrows doubtfully.

"I wouldn't have thought so. Nor," Davie added after a pause, "would I have thought that they would covet the Europa. By the way, Mr. Vanásek had only just acquired it. He told me that morning that I was the first person he'd shown it to."

"This bit of china complicates everything. A thief might have picked it up on the spur of the moment, but if no one else knew it was there it couldn't have been an original motive for the attack."

"Oh yes it could," said Davie. "Mr. Vanásek had bought it at an auction. Many people who know about these things would know that he had it."

"Well—we can check on these musicians as easily as on anybody else. But as for that china group—what use is it to anyone? If it's famous it's impossible to sell. China's not like jewellery."

"Not a bit. But a thief, an odd sort of thief, might just want to keep it."

"A collector thief?"

"Yes," said Davie. "There are such people."

"Who commit murder for it?"

"Who do not mean to commit murder."

"This man meant what he did," said Tabor, remembering the bruised neck of Jiří Vanásek.

Then he lowered his sights and with deliberate precision arranged a ruler, a pencil, and an india rubber, in an isosceles triangle on the blotting pad. And, "Yes," he said. "That's the point."

"Is there anything else—" began Davie.

"Not at the minute, sir. You're at the King William?"

"Yes."

"Please don't go away. There'll be the inquest. Thursday, I would think. It will be a brief business. Almost certainly a postponement."

"I was expecting to be here for the week," said Davie, rising.

"Good," said Tabor. "Goodbye, Dr. Davie. Thank you."

IV

Halfway between the police station and the King William stands the shop of Mr. Coombes, clockmaker and jeweller. Davie had often observed that rotund and beaming figure standing at his open door, amiably engaged in doing nothing at all, and he had often wondered how Mr. Coombes, or any other of his trade, existed. He could not sell many clocks; and surely his trade in jewellery was minimal—except for occasional engagement rings and the ultimate gold circle of surrender. But did anyone buy the napkin rings, toast racks, pickle forks, lucky silver charms, birth stones, tea knives, vases, and all the figures of doggies, guardsmen, beefeaters, and Queen Elizabeth, which filled the main part of the window?

Davie paused to examine Mr. Coombes's offerings, his attention particularly engaged by a picture of an old world cottage garden so close to the sea that it seemed highly improbable that any of its luxuriant flowers could survive the wild salt winds. It's like one of those competition pictures, he was thinking. Spot the mistakes. Send in your entry with three tops of "Snow Queen" soap powder, Prize £1,000. And, he went on, warming to his project, five thousand consolation prizes of "Snow Queen" soap powder. . . . If the tulips are right, then the hollyhocks are wrong; the sunflowers—

And there the fantasy faded. Davie's attention was distracted. A man had appeared in the open doorway, saying, "Now mind, Mr. Coombes—"

"You don't trust me," said the beaming Mr. Coombes.

"Not an inch," said the man. "Last time you said a week—"

"Ah—but, sir! That was the mainspring—"

"All right—but I'm lost without it. Which reminds me, what *is* the time, as of now?"

"Well . . . ," said Mr. Coombes, turning his head towards the shelf behind his glass counter, where several clocks stood, stopped or ticking, at a variety of times. "Well . . . I would say, sir—"

At the far end of High Street the great clock of St. Stephen's began to chime.

"I would say it was a quarter past ten, sir," said Mr. Coombes, "and it's going to be another fine day, I do believe."

"You're an old fraud," said the man.

110

"It will be ready by Saturday," said Mr. Coombes with an enormous smile. "I promise you that, Mr. Major."

"It better had," said the man, getting into his car.

He drove off in the direction of Bexminster. And, yes, thought Davie, that was the chap who was talking to Rowan and Caske after lunch on Sunday. Clegg said it would be Mr. Major.

Not that it mattered. But Davie liked having things straight in his mind. He returned to the King William.

In the hall Richard Serpent, Jack Pincock, and several Festival visitors were busy talking about Robert Coppleston. Davie walked past them into the lounge where, round the corner, out of sight of the door, Mildred Meade-Fuller, Mrs. Mapleton-Morley, and Miss Bangle were heads together on the same subject. There was no retreat.

"Have you heard the terrible news?" said Mrs. Mapleton-Morley.

"Yes," said Davie, "I've heard it—but you can be sure that no one's story at this stage is correct."

"Battered to death!" said Mrs. Mapleton-Morley. "Unrecognizable!"

"Is that what you heard?"

"In Combe Magna!" said Mildred Meade-Fuller.

Miss Bangle did not speak: she raised her eyebrows and glanced upwards as who should say for heaven's sake change the subject for us.

"I'll tell you something that *is* correct," said Davie. "The weather's going to change—I'm sure of it."

"The weather, R.V.!" said Mildred Meade-Fuller. "Must you?"

"I don't know why not. It's interesting. We are so privileged. People who live in climates where conditions are boringly predictable don't talk about the weather. Naturally not. You don't come down to breakfast in the middle of the Indian monsoon and say 'Oh dear! Another wet day!' And on the hurricane coast of America you don't exhibit surprise at being blown into the harbour at regular intervals—but in this blessed plot, this England, when it suddenly hails in June or contrariwise when crocuses come up by mistake in December, it's a matter for comment. Truly I'd rather talk about the weather than the balance of payments—"

"But we weren't talking about the balance of payments, R.V.," said Mildred Meade-Fuller.

"You are being sarcastic with us," said Mrs. Mapleton-Morley, wagging a much beringed finger.

"I hope not. That's a terribly boring tone of voice. Satire's all right. He's a serious man. Wit's all right: he sees the point and he's quick on the draw. Irony's all right: he's brave: he's only armed with his tongue. But Sarcasm! Stupid, boring, obvious, furious Sarcasm! He goes around waving what the police call a blunt instrument. He's greatly respected in the prep school, and in the House of Commons."

"Well done, R.V.," said Mildred Meade-Fuller. "Quite like old times. I gather you were not being sarcastic."

"No, truly: as I was saying—"

"When we so rudely interrupted you."

"I'd rather talk about the weather than the balance of payments—"

"That's where we came in: I remember."

"Or these ghastly murders."

"Murders, R.V.?"

"Murders," said Davie. "You'll hear all about it soon enough. Meantime—the weather is better, and safer. Believe me, Mildred, much safer. . . . Forgive me," he added: "there's Frederick Dyke. I must catch him."

Looking back from the door, he saw Mrs. Mapleton-

Morley droop her head towards Mildred Meade-Fuller and make a wide gesture with both hands. She was saying in a low voice, "What's the matter with the man?" But Miss Bangle was looking directly at him. Very plainly she shut up one eye in an enormous wink. Davie approved of Miss Bangle.

V

Madame Jeanne, Hairstyles, née Shirley Muffin, was a nice ordinary young woman in her late twenties—though she looked older because she had thought well to bleach one of her dark locks a silver grey. Her lady customers considered this smart, and so did Shirley, but the more simple men of King's Lacy thought it was hard luck that a nice girl like Shirley should go grey so prematurely. They did not know that women make up not to attract men but to stun other women. Girls think they can best defeat the men with their hidden weapons. And they are right: only a very pure young man falls for a woman's face.

Born and brought up in Bexminster, Miss Muffin had had a year's training in a shop in Bournemouth, and having in so short a time (in the estimation of her teachers, for she had a framed certificate declaring their confidence in her proficiency) acquired an art which has baffled the witches of many thousand years, the art of making ugly women beautiful, she had set up her salon, behind nylon curtains looped with pink ribbons, in a handsome old house next door to the King William and immediately opposite to George's; and no one in King's Lacy had a better opportunity than she for observing the comings and goings in High Street, for, unlike many shopkeepers, Madame Jeanne lived over her work. During the day she spent her time on the ground floor, but even as she attended the heads and faces of her clients, she always managed to keep an eye on the window. She enjoyed watching the world of King's Lacy from behind her nylon defenses, and thinking about Jiří Vanásek's visitors while she yanked out Mrs. Sage's eyebrows, or placed a pack on the perspiring face of Janice Perriam.

"There's that Mr. Coppleston," she would say to herself, "funny he isn't married"—and then, out loud, "I do hope it will keep fine for the church fête," or "Did you see the play on television last night? It really was good," or sometimes "I don't like repeating things, but—" for Madame Jeanne was an expert at adapting her conversation to the interests of her clients.

After six o'clock Madame Jeanne had an even better view of the world from the first floor room, which was used during the day as a waiting room and after business hours was converted into "the lounge," though the shining hardness of the linoleum and the forbidding texture of the rexine-covered furniture was powerfully against any abandonment to luxury.

It was in this room that Madame Jeanne was receiving Inspector Tabor and a satellite constable at half past ten o'clock on Monday morning. She would be happy to help in any way she could, said Madame Jeanne, and indeed she was very pleased to be consulted, though glad, too, that a cancellation had ensured that there would be no embarrassment with her clients. She had no booking now till eleven, and Betty, her assistant priestess, could look after the shop until then.

"Your name—" began Tabor.

"Madame Jeanne, Hair—"

"I mean your real name."

"Oh!" said Madame Jeanne, colouring slightly, "Muffin, Shirley Muffin."

On Saturday evening, said Miss Muffin, she had been upstairs with her friend, here, in the lounge.

"Your friend?"

"Jack Crumble—you know, the son of Mr. Crumble, the Lady's shop."

"Yes, yes."

"But we were watching the television—well, most of the time we were," said Miss Muffin suddenly blushing as she remembered a period on the sofa when she hadn't been watching the telly at all for at least twenty minutes.

"I am only anxious to find out if you happened to see anyone at any time entering or leaving George's," said Tabor.

"Well, yes," said Miss Muffin. "After my friend had gone, when I was tidying up, I did happen to look out of the window at about half past eleven, and Mr. Vanásek was standing at his door saying goodbye to somebody. He waited till the person had gone across the road to the King William, and then he went in."

"Could you see if he locked the door?"

"Well, not for sure I couldn't, no. That would be having eyes like telescopes—but he did stand for a few seconds inside the door—you know—like he would if he was locking it."

"I see."

Tabor made a note that Mr. Vanásek probably had locked his door—which was what one would naturally have supposed. This was nothing new, nothing certain.

But Miss Muffin, who had got over her embarrassment, had more to say.

"I went downstairs to make myself some tea and I was

down there longer than I meant because there were things to do. You know how it is. And then I went upstairs to bed. I had to go into the lounge because I hadn't turned the telly off, and then I went across to the window, and there was Mr. Vanásek at his door again. He came out and shut it and went down the little alley at the side. It was late for a walk, but it was a lovely night and Mr. Vanásek was always a bit—you know—different."

"What time was this?"

"Just after twelve. The clock was striking in the kitchen as I came up. It was late for me."

"Did you notice if he locked the door that time?"

"I don't think he did," said Miss Muffin. "Not double lock. But the door would have shut on the Yale."

Tabor made another note in his book. Then, without looking up, he asked, "You're sure it was Mr. Vanásek?"

"Why yes," said Miss Muffin, astonished. "It couldn't have been anyone else at that time of night, could it?"

Tabor did not pursue the matter, but asked if she had seen anyone else at all.

"Well, not Sunday, because I went down to the sea with my friend, and I didn't see anyone there in the evening."

"So, since Saturday night, you've seen no one else at any time enter the shop?"

"Well—this morning," said Miss Muffin with a knowing smile, "naturally I did. There was you and the elderly gentleman at twenty past nine. And before that, there was Mrs. Bazeley. She often goes to see Mr. Vanásek and usually early—she's got her own business to attend to. The door wasn't open though, and she went away down the alley. I expect she was going to Mr. Vanásek's back door."

"What time was that?"

"A quarter to nine."

"Isn't George's usually open at that time?"

"Yes—half past eight, always. Mr. Vanásek was late."

"Anyone else?"

"There was one man went down the alley soon after Mrs. Bazeley. He came back again about two minutes later. He might have been calling on Mr. Vanásek. I don't know."

"Can you describe him?"

"Not really. I didn't see his face. He'd got a hat on and I was upstairs."

Tabor looked down at his notes, tapped his nose several times with his pencil and so got up and took his leave.

"Thank you, Miss Muffin. You have been very helpful."

"I'm glad. Is that all?"

"Yes, thank you. I am obliged to you."

And, "That young woman doesn't miss much," said Tabor to the constable when they were back in the car. "Now, where does this Mrs. Bazeley hang out?"

But Mrs. Bazeley was not able to help at all. "Yes," she said, "I did call at George's this morning early. The shop was shut, so I went round to the side door. I rang the bell, and then as there wasn't any answer, I opened the door."

"It wasn't bolted?"

"No. So I knew he couldn't be far off. I waited a minute and called out. But there was no answer, and I couldn't wait. He must have gone out."

"He wasn't out, Mrs. Bazeley."

"Not out? Where was he?"

"In the office."

"In the office? But—"

"You know the room?"

"Of course: I've been in it scores of times."

"You didn't go in this morning?"

It would not have been possible for Mrs. Bazeley to

change colour—but she looked suddenly anxious, and raised three crimson fingernails nervously to her lips.

"Is there anything the matter?"

"There is, indeed, Mrs. Bazeley."

"Not—"

"Mr. Vanásek is dead."

"I—" began Mrs. Bazeley, and suddenly fell backwards on a chair—which was not at all characteristic behaviour in Mrs. Bazeley.

VI

There is a room on the first floor of the King William Hotel marked "Drawing room. Residents Only," and thither Davie made his way after escaping from Mrs. Mapleton-Morley. As he expected, the room was empty. In the evening there would have been two or three commercial travellers filling in reports and orders, two old ladies knitting, and a mysterious couple talking in low voices in a corner. But nobody wanted the drawing room in the morning, indeed up to half past ten it was always occupied by a whirling carpet sweeper. But now, at a quarter to eleven, all was tidy, the windows were closed, and the room had already regained its ancient smell, compounded of curtains, chintz, and the distant memory of last night's tobacco.

On a table against a wall was a pile of old magazines, and, promising better things, four covers embossed with the names of respected publications. Davie picked up the one named *Punch*, lowered himself into a chintz-covered chair, and prepared to be amused. Inside the cover was a copy of *The Motor*. To Davie, who had never driven a car in his life, this was a peculiar affront. He shut the cover with a snap, closed his eyes, and leaned back in his chair. Was there ever such a blatantly false clue as that? And he had fallen for it. False clues can muddy up an entire investigation. On the other hand, when a false clue is detected it turns into a dangerously real clue pointing in an opposite direction.

Beware of false clues, thought Dr. Davie, putting his hand in his side pocket. Yes—there was the post, one letter and three circulars. Horrid circulars, beastly circulars, he had thought at breakfast. But now he had kindlier feelings towards them. Three splendid circulars they were, with three large empty backs. Even the lying cover of the alleged *Punch* had revealed a new purpose. On his lap it made a table.

Davie felt in his breast pocket and produced a pen.

ROBERT COPPLESTON [he wrote] is killed after making and attempting to keep an appointment with William Carroll. He said—I heard him say—that he would set off at once. That means either that he was followed or that he was intercepted. As he was on a bicycle he could very easily have been followed in a car, or passed by a car and later waylaid. It looks as though he were attacked as he entered the drive at Combe Court. But he could have been attacked somewhere outside and brought there. The bicycle, indeed, must have been carried to where it was found. Coppleston was not riding among the rhododendrons.

It was a good place to hide the body. Apparently—so Tabor said—it was discovered by pure accident. Carroll's car lights caught the glint of the handlebars through the hedge.

Coppleston was carrying a bit of paper which had been concealed in the Worcester sugar bowl. But if that is what his attacker wanted he did not find it. It had got into his coat lining. Presumably this was what Coppleston wanted to show William Carroll. But he might have been carrying something else, and perhaps his attacker did get what he wanted. I don't think so. His pockets ransacked; his possessions scattered on the ground; it suggests a desperate search.

But how, so quickly, was the murderer alerted? That is the heart of the matter. Vanásek might have seen Coppleston take the paper. Someone outside the shop might have seen him. Someone in a house opposite might have seen something. But surely the more probable explanation is that someone overheard the telephone call. It seems unlikely that the wire would be tapped. The only other possibility seems to be that the conversation, or enough of it, was heard by someone in the hall. That there was someone in the hall before I entered it is almost certain—because of the slowly closing door to the lounge. There were about twenty people in the lounge. It is curious that the only three I can identify—Rowan, Caske, and Major—are all directors of Coppleston's firm. I haven't the smallest reason to suspect any of them, and indeed know nothing about any of them—except that the first two play golf, and the third is an occasional customer of Mr. Coombes.

This isn't much—but two things seem to me important. The note. And the door.

Davie drew a heavy line across the page and stared across the room at a small shelf of books—a collection typical of all country hotels—the local guide books mixed up with visitors' leavings and one or two volumes that had once belonged to the grandfather of some forgotten proprietor. *Historical Bexminster* stood between *The Carpetbaggers* and *David Copperfield. A Guide to Bexminster Abbey* was supported by *Under Two Flags, The Guns of Navarone,* and two volumes of *The Strand Magazine.*

Davie made a mental note that he must take *The Strand* to bed with him. Then he began writing again.

JIRI VANASEK was undoubtedly scared of the Czech musicians, but, it seems to me for very little reason. Artists are not the murderer type, and the accidental betrayal by a child is surely not a matter for such a savage revenge. But of course there may be something here that I don't know.

The fact that Coppleston's paper had been hidden in Vanásek's bowl appears to connect the two deaths. It is also a fact that the two men were killed in much the same way. If the note were a message that had got into the wrong hands, if its discovery were likely to lead to some disastrous disclosure, if there were someone who couldn't allow the note to be lost, and couldn't allow it to be found either—at least not by the wrong person—then that person may have felt that killing was the only way out.

Jiří appears to have been an agent of some kind. He allowed his shop to be used as a post office. Spies do use intermediaries. One might think they could as easily make calls, write letters, or telephone. Certainly they could—and run the risk of being seen, read, heard. An intermediary is good sense. It saves the important two from meeting.

But there's always the risk that the third party may not play straight—and equally a risk for the third party who does not play straight. Something happens to him. Something happened to Jiří Vanásek.

I do not think he would have let a stranger in at that time of night. Assuming that he later locked the front door, I think the murderer must have got in at the back door while we were saying goodnight at the front. We had been sitting outside. And we were not whispering. If anyone had been at the gate and intent on hearing, he could have heard, and after we left he could have guessed that the door was open.

Davie paused, and gazed across at the King William library again. But this time he did not see the titles. He was saying to himself—"but that means, that means . . ."

The last of the circulars was an invitation from a Unit Trust warmly suggesting that Davie should entrust his all to their expert administration. He turned it over and wrote eight lines more on its broad white back:

Our conversation was about the tragedy in Czechoslovakia. Not about anything else. Perhaps those Czechs are not such a long shot. What else were we talking about that could have aroused anyone's fear or hate? . . . What else? Begin again! In the last three minutes we were talking about spying and blackmail. If that part had been overheard by the right person

121

one could begin to see the point. Still, on Jiří's own word the Czechs are not to be forgotten.

Then Dr. Davie drew another line. He had been writing for an hour and felt tired. He closed his eyes.

A minute later he opened them again.

THE EUROPA [he wrote]—there is that third problem. Who stole the Europa? And did he murder Jiří Vanásek? It's possible. But surely he didn't murder Coppleston too? It's a curious thought, though, that Coppleston was a collector of china. But so is Sir Philip Gossamer.

Then Dr. Davie put his pen away, folded his papers and put them in his pocket. He was indeed tired. He closed his eyes, and this time he fell asleep.

VII

After dinner that night Davie made his way to the bar. He had felt quite unable to listen to madrigals in the hall of the old Grammar School. He did not do much bar-leaning as a rule. But Joe Major was there and Davie wanted to speak to him.

These King's Lacy crimes were no affair of his. He'd soon be told to mind his own business if he started rooting round, asking questions, looking for clues. But, as always, he was curious, and his sympathy was engaged. He had liked Jiří Vanásek: the man had confided in him. Irresistibly he wanted to do something for his ghost. And since Mr. Major lived opposite to Jiří's garden wall he felt there might be something he had seen, something he had heard, something that might cast some kind of glimmer on the tragedy. Of course Tabor would have asked him all the right questions already. But Davie didn't see why he shouldn't ask his own. Provided it was on a friendly basis.

He sidled up to the bar and asked for a glass of port. The room was loud with talk and everyone was talking about the same thing. No one was inhibited by ignorance from expressing an opinion, because everyone had been told something by somebody and could therefore pose as a repository of proven fact.

Taking no part in the conversation, Joe Major was sitting alone at the end of the counter. There was a space beside him and Davie moved into it.

They exchanged a "good evening." And then Davie said, "There's only one topic of conversation tonight," and somehow he managed to convey that he and, he politely presumed, Joe Major, were above that sort of thing.

"Yes," said Joe Major, turning his glass of whisky slowly round on the bar top. "Yes. I happened to know both of them—one well, and one enough to pass the time of day with."

"I knew Vanásek," said Davie.

"He was the one I only knew slightly. My house is just beyond George's back garden wall. So of course we saw each other from time to time."

"Am I right in thinking you are Mr. Major?" said Davie.

"Yes."

"My name is Davie. I'm here for the Festival."

"And you know my name?"

"You were pointed out to me as the owner of a splendid collection of paperweights."

"Really? I didn't know they were that famous. Are you a collector?"

"No—but I have a few. I like them very much—so long as they aren't those vulgar bogus ones."

Then Davie began talking about the making of paperweights.

"It's rather like the mystery of putting a ship in a bottle. It looks miraculous, but there's a rational explanation. If you hold one up to your eye, you can sometimes see the join."

It was not long before Joe Major was saying, "My place is only a step away. If you're interested, do come and look at them."

Half an hour later, the subject of paperweights exhausted, the two men were sitting in the lamplight talking about Jiří Vanásek and Robert Coppleston. On the table between them were two glasses, a jug of water, and a bottle of whisky.

"There is a curious link between the two cases," Davie was saying. "A piece of paper that had been in the possession of Vanásek, was afterwards found on the body of Coppleston. I happen to know what that paper was because I've seen it twice—once by accident in Vanásek's shop—it was lying in a sugar bowl—and once, two days later at the police station. It had been found in the lining of Coppleston's jacket."

Davie paused, as if a little uncertain how much further to go. Joe Major eyed him curiously: almost he looked as though he had guessed that Dr. Davie's encounter with him in the King William bar had not been entirely accidental.

"And what did it say, this paper?" said Joe Major.

"It gave two dates."

"Two dates, eh?"

"Yes—8.9 and 29.9."

There was no shadow of change on Joe Major's face, but ten seconds went by before he spoke.

"And that's all?"

"That's all. Do you make anything of it?"

Joe Major replied with a counter question.

"Do you suppose the police will have asked William Carroll that question?"

"I would have thought so. They know Coppleston wanted

124

to see Carroll about something. They would probably ask him if this paper could have had anything to do with it. If he should recognize its significance—"

"He would," said Joe Major shortly.

Davie waited.

"Look here, sir," said Joe Major, "this is a difficult subject for me. But if these dates are in the hands of the police they are bound to learn what they mean, so perhaps I shall not be indiscreet if I tell you."

"I'd be very grateful if you would."

"But will you promise not to discuss the matter with any-one else—unless it be the police?"

"Yes," said Davie, "I will promise that."

"Those dates are very private dates concerned with the production program of Bexminster Electronics. They were only decided on Friday. And within twenty-four hours they are in the hands of this Vanásek. Was he a spy, or what? It's plain enough to me. Coppleston got to know of this message and started off to report to William Carroll. Someone didn't want that to happen."

"But Mr. Major—two murders for a couple of dates! Does that make sense?"

"Yes, sir, it does. Because the dates wouldn't be the point. You see, Dr. Davie, there have been betrayals at Bexminster Electronics before. Possibly several times, twice certainly, trade secrets of ours have been leaked to Japan. At the present time we're doing high security work on Government contract. You may think those dates trivial—I don't—but suppose they are—"

"Yes?"

"Well, find the person who betrayed a couple of dates and you will certainly find the person who fiddled with greater matters. That person can't risk that. It is of no consequence whether the offense concerns a sheep or lamb. He does not intend to be caught for either."

"I see. I didn't know. That puts a new light on the whole thing. I don't want to be curious about your affairs, But I am concerned for Vanásek's sake. I can't forestall the police—but I do wish I could satisfy my own mind. Someone was using Vanásek."

"Evidently."

For a few seconds both men stared at the carpet. Then Davie said, "Did no one but the directors and Coppleston know these dates?"

"No one except Miss Jesmond, the Board's secretary. She knows everything about all of us. You might have seen her. She lives on the top of Madame Jeanne's, next door to the King William."

"You can trust her?"

"As soon as anyone."

"But the fact remains that there must have been a leak in high places."

"That's the ghastly and incredible thing. Unless there's a spy operating on the premises—which I doubt—there must have been a leak . . . in high places, which I find equally hard to swallow."

"Were you at home that night?"

"Yes—well, after eleven I was."

"Did you see nothing? Hear nothing? At Vanásek's I mean."

"I didn't come home down the alley. I'd walked along High Street, talking to someone—and then I turned down Baggot Avenue and came up Brook Lane. That was about eleven. I think I did hear voices as I passed the end of Vanásek's garden."

"That was Vanásek and I. No—I mean later—after half past eleven."

"I didn't hear anything or see anything. I was working. And my window doesn't have a view of Vanásek's gate—only of the garden back wall and of the start of the alley in Brook Lane. Very few people use the alley late at night. One person came down it—twenty-five past eleven I think it was—and that was William Carroll. He'd driven one of the Czechs to the Bear after the concert and drinks at Lacy. Then he called on me, and went home at about ten to twelve. And oddly enough, if you're brooding over alibis for improbable people, he was at his home a quarter of an hour later. I know because I rang him up."

"Why?" asked Davie—aware that he was being blunt, but anxious to know.

"He'd dropped his ring—and I knew he'd worry about it. I was right. He said he wouldn't have lost it for a wilderness of monkeys."

"A literary man."

"Indeed yes. He and Philip Gossamer provide the civilized strains in Bexminster Electronics. And perhaps Alec Rowan. I and Daniel Caske are the barbarians."

Davie looked round the room. "A barbarian with some taste."

"In paperweights—but my life has really been devoted to mathematics. And, of course, girls."

"There is art in both pursuits," said Davie, getting up. "I'm sure I should be going. What's the time?"

"Now that's something I won't know till next Saturday," said Joe Major. "And I dare say not then. Coombes is an old rogue and never keeps his word. I have a famous clock that goes like a lamb for months—except that it's usually fast. But sometimes, when I dare to regulate it, it stops for no reason that I know, not being a clockmaker, and sometimes it doesn't mind. Sometimes it packs up on its own. I spent a large part of Sunday thinking I'd got up very late and then I

127

found it had stopped just before twelve on Saturday night. I've had to rely on St. Stephen ever since. But of course *he* packs up at night, and then I've no idea at all. I rather like it."

"Well—I was being lazy," said Davie. "I do have a watch in the recesses of my waistcoat. Here it is. Eleven-forty. Late for me."

"Not for me."

"So I understand. Thank you very much for showing me these pretty things, for my drink, and for your interesting information and confidence."

"Not at all. I've enjoyed talking with you. Only two steps to the path. Don't fall into the brook. There is a rail on the bridge."

For a few moments Davie lingered on the bridge, watching the water flow beneath his feet. Age is constantly occupied with memory. He had only to look at the water and the forget-me-nots and he was sixty-five years away, squatting beside a brook that flowed incontinently across a lane on its journey between two fields, and he in his holland pinafore sailing paper boats. A brook crossing a road was nothing in those days. The horses splashed through it and the boys launched boats on it and ran across the field in the fervid expectation that the boats would survive eddies and weeds and branches and stones, hazards equivalent to those awaiting larger vessels in the vicinity of Cape Horn.

So much to remember in ten seconds!

A cigarette carton came bobbing down the stream, catching on a weed, freeing itself, sailing on again. Davie hastily looked over the rail on the other side for the childish pleasure of seeing it arrive; and when it didn't he leaned over the rail and tried to see what had happened to it. And then the carton, having unhitched itself from some obstacle, came floating down, nobly breasting the wave. He did not approve of rubbish in a brook—but this rubbish was behaving like a boat; and he couldn't help wishing it well.

But this was absurd. He stepped into Brook Lane and walked up the alley by George's shop in the darkness. Two nights before at about the same time a murderer had entered this alley, had opened Jiří Vanásek's garden gate, and had walked into the house while he and Jiří were saying goodbye at the front door. Of that he felt certain.

Eleven-fifty was not late for the King William in Festival week. Davie could hear voices in the lounge talking about the second performance of *The Fairies*.

Not in the mood for that, he mounted the oak staircase, decided in passing that he was against copper warming pans and brass skimmers, in favour of blue and white china, coloured maps and playbills, and made his way along an irregular corridor to his panelled bedroom at the back of the house. It was variously alleged that Charles II, on the run, Judge Jeffreys, and William of Orange, had occupied this room. Well, so they might have done, Davie used to think—but their proprietary rights were surely diminished by Time. The point was that the room was now occupied by Dr. R. V. Davie. All its amenities, such as they were, were for his sole pleasure. And for the same admirable purpose there lay upon his bedside table Volume 2 of *The Strand Magazine*, June to December 1891.

Slowly he went through the unalterable routine of undressing. Keys, coins, wallet, spectacles, engagement book, handkerchief: then coat and trousers on hangers in the wardrobe. It all followed like clockwork. But before getting into bed at once, as he usually did, he sat down at his

129

dressing table, and thought about Joe Major and his paper-weights, twinkling pink and blue and green in the subdued light of his bachelor's study. All those girls! For Joe Major had told all: no regretted expenditure of spirit as far as he was concerned, and no nonsense about a waste of shame either. Davie was staggered at the extent of his amorous operations, and delighted by the paperweights. But he had learned nothing at all about Jiří Vanásek.

Only one thing he did wonder about a little, and that was Joe Major's statement that William Carroll had come down the alley at eleven twenty-five. And Joe Major had said that his clock was usually fast. He and Jiří were still in the garden then and surely they would have heard him. And then he remembered that Jiří had stopped and listened at about that time—but neither of them had heard anything. If William Carroll had gone down the alley at eleven twenty-five it must have been on tiptoe. But of course he might have gone down it a minute or two later and they'd have been indoors. It sounded pernickety and unimportant, but to the curious all things are curious, and that was the thought that passed through Davie's mind as he sat there staring at his hair brushes.

Presently, lifting his eyes to the looking glass Davie found himself contemplating the white hospitable reaches of his bed, the sheet invitingly turned down to welcome him. And there in the glass was *The Strand Magazine*. Davie dismissed his problems instantly, picked up his spectacles, skipped into bed, snuggled himself into the perfect position with the aid of the third pillow he had begged from Maggie, the chambermaid, and opened the honoured volume at a page already selected earlier in the day.

Judge Jeffreys be damned: he held in his hands the first publication of *The Red-Headed League* by A. Conan Doyle.

Tuesday

I

DAVIE COUNTED THE STROKES OF THE GREAT CLOCK OF ST. Stephen's. Four, five, six, seven. Seven o'clock. The mystery of *The Red-Headed League* successfully resolved, he had slept well, without thinking more about his own problems. But now they came back to him afresh. Why hadn't they heard Mr. Carroll going down the alley at eleven-twenty-five, or perhaps eleven-twenty? Obvious answer: because he hadn't gone down it at that time. Mr. Major had made a mistake. Last night the point had not seemed particularly important. In the light of early morning, shining pink through thin flowered curtains, the discrepancy wore another look. If someone entered the garden at eleven-thirty he must have been hanging around for a bit before—waiting for the clear moment and incidentally hearing what he and Vanásek were saying. If William Carroll had come down the alley at eleven twenty-five he would almost certainly have run into him. He would even have been able to identify him, perhaps, and he surely must have told the police about it.

If he had not seen anyone then he must have come down the passage later than Joe Major had believed. It only had to be four or five minutes later and the story could be acceptable, and no doubt that was the explanation. But it was tantalizing. Carroll must have been so nearly in the right place at the right time. It was only at just about eleven-thirty that an intruder could have entered Jiří's garden. William Carroll might have come down the passage at eleven thirty-one and seen no one.

All this was conjecture. What wasn't conjecture was that Carroll and Major had been together at about that time, and did not part till nearly twelve; and that a quarter of an hour later they had been speaking on the telephone, Major in Brook Lane, Carroll in Combe Magna. It was all tidy except for that clock—eleven twenty-five, and Joe Major said it was usually fast.

Davie sat up in bed, swivelled around, groped for his slippers with pendant toes, padded over to the window and drew the curtains. It was another lovely day. Good. His prognostications of a change in the weather had been totally inaccurate. Then he entered the bathroom, turned on the taps and started to shave.

Who else had been abroad that night? he was thinking. Sir Philip Gossamer: he'd driven three Czechs to the Bear. Where had he gone after that? Where had the Czechs gone? Where were Mr. Caske and Mr. Rowan? Where were all the citizens of King's Lacy? The police would know the answer to these questions. But he, Dr. R. V. Davie, did not. If he were going to do any thinking he'd have to do it on his own. He was an outsider this time. Not thinking for anyone. But why hadn't Mr. Carroll seen somebody? Because he'd really come through a bit later. And why hadn't he and Jiří heard him? Because he'd really come through a bit later. The thought went over and over in his mind. It got him nowhere. It was vexing.

For a few minutes Davie switched his attention to the knobs and furrows of the familiar face in the glass—the face that was his the wrong way round. With his hair in three grey peaks like Pantaloon he thought he looked depressingly ancient and wholly unattractive: but by the time he'd dolled himself up, and doused his hair with Eau de Portugal, he had hopes that he would pass for sixty-two . . . well, sixty-five. It was strange, but these things mattered to Dr. Davie. And, oh dear . . . the false clue, he was thinking, as he rubbed in the Eau de Portugal. I'm *The Motor* masquerading in the covers of *Punch*.

Dr. Davie finished his dressing and went downstairs to breakfast. He had decided to pay two calls. One was a matter of private business: that would be easy. The other— he really had no idea how the other would go.

II

The nearly spherical Mr. Coombes was standing in his shop door surveying the world of King's Lacy with an enormous smile upon his face. He seemed to consider himself excused on this beautiful morning from doing any of the boring work which awaited him in the dark little room at the back of the shop: there was nothing that couldn't stay until tomorrow, and he would really be very put out indeed if anyone brought him anything new. A pickle fork, now, or a figure of Queen Elizabeth—that would be different, but it wasn't often that anyone wanted one of those. Mr. Coombes considered himself pretty safe for the day.

He was, therefore, not very pleased when he observed an elderly gentleman approaching along the pavement with that look in his eye which suggested that Mr. Coombes's shop was the end and object of his expedition: and, indeed, the gentleman came straight up to him and said, "Good morning. May I come in? I'd like to look at a watch."

It had occurred to Dr. Davie that a seventh birthday was coming up for Abel Courtney, youngest of the Master's children at St. Nicholas's College. A watch would be a good idea; and, indeed, Mr. Coombes was not ill-disposed to consider the sale of a watch. He had not hoped for anything as simple as that.

And so, the choice made and the sale completed, there they were, Dr. Davie and Mr. Coombes, in close confabulation across the counter on the subject of watches and clocks, and how to look after them.

"The boy's only seven," said Davie. "He'll break it if he possibly can. Are there any special things I ought to tell him?"

"No," said Mr. Coombes. "Except not to drop it on the floor, and not to put it in his bath, and not to hit it with a cricket bat—but otherwise nothing in particular."

"I had an idea that you mustn't put clocks and watches back."

"That's striking clocks," said Mr. Coombes. "And even then only when the hands are in a particular position. Suppose a clock's pointing at a quarter to the hour and you put it back to a quarter past the previous hour—that wouldn't necessarily hurt it, not if it were an English clock, striking the hours only. But if you put it back when it stood at four minutes past the hour—no matter if it was put back five minutes or thirty-five minutes, it would stop when it got back to about four minutes before the hour—the time when the strike gets itself ready. It would stop, you see, because it's already struck the hour once and it don't want to do it again—the lifting piece would be out of position, distorted, stuck. I've got a clock here that's done just that. Gentleman brought it in yesterday. Thought he'd put it right before going to bed, I expect, and all he done were to stop it altogether."

"You'd have thought people with a striking clock would know that."

"Ah," said Mr. Coombes, shaking his head, "you'd think people would know a lot of things they don't."

As Davie walked down the street towards St. Stephen's, on the sunny side of the road, he went on thinking about clocks. He didn't doubt Mr. Coombes had been talking about Joe Major's clock, and he couldn't help working it out. Evidently, after William Carroll had gone home—probably immediately after Joe telephoned about the ring—Joe Major had decided to adjust his increasingly fast clock, and had put it back, whatever it needed, five minutes, ten minutes, and in doing so had pushed the hand back past the hour, with the result that, not long after, the "lifting piece," as Mr. Coombes had called it, had stuck.

Did that fact have any bearing upon the time that William Carroll came down the alley? Not exactly, because he came down the alley before the clock was put back. But Mr. Coombes's information did have some bearing on the problem. Clearly, the clock *was* fast, or Joe wouldn't have put it back: and that meant that when Carroll arrived at eleven twenty-five the real time might well have been eleven-twenty or even earlier. It was unsatisfactory to know that he and Vanásek ought to have heard William Carroll as he walked down the alley on his way to call on Joe Major. Davie did not like being confronted with facts that he couldn't understand. He still presumed that Joe Major had made a mistake. William Carroll had perhaps come down the alley at eleven thirty-five.

And there he was at St. Stephen's. With so much to distract him he had neglected too many of the delights of King's Lacy. He had been in the town four days and he had not yet visited his favourite church. He pushed open the door and entered that noble nave, executed in the superb honey-coloured stone of Ham Hill. There was nobody else there. He stood in the center aisle and looked down the length of the church to the east window, and upwards to the mighty fan-vaulted roof. What larks they must have had in building it! Those faces on the corbels, were they portraits of the monks, or portraits of the masons, or portraits of important citizens? And that one with his tongue out, was he a demon or a rude boy from the monastery school? Davie liked to think he was the same boy who was exhibited on one of the carved miserere seats in the choir, being soundly birched by an irate usher. Truly St. Stephen's was a humorous edifice, intentionally and unintentionally. Even the eighteenth-century monuments, which fitted ill with the fifteenth-century building, were dear for their own sakes: those proud bewigged faces, those Muses grieving beside Grecian urns, the marmoreal tears of corpulent cherubs.

Only one thing distressed the eye. Someone at the nadir of taste in the last century had painted the commandments in blue and red and gold on the transept wall. But even that, in time, might fade into beauty, and add something for the future to admire, as sometimes we uncover, and profess to admire, some mighty strange decorations of the past. Or so Davie speculated as he opened the padded door and stepped again into the sunshine.

From the church he strolled down Stephen's Row and peered through the window at "Treasure Trove" and thence moved on to Baggot Street to take a look at "Odds and Ends" and "The Curio Cupboard." So far as he could see old mother Snaresbrook's cupboard was uncommonly bare. So he turned out of Baggot Street, crossed Baggot Avenue, and found himself at the bottom of Brook Lane at the point where the brook had been encased, and condemned by man to travel underground until, conveniently to him, it emerges again in the water meadows outside the town.

Davie walked along Brook Lane and presently arrived at the little bridge that led across the water to Joe Major's house. And there he stopped and looked first at the house on his right which he had visited on Monday night, and then to the left, across the road, to Jiří Vanásek's garden wall. In that house a man had been murdered. In this one a man had been sitting up, working by an open window on a still night: and he knew nothing about it. True, murderers do not advertise; but Mr. Major's unawareness was nevertheless a matter of interest.

Davie always had to bother his head with some problem, but the alley beside George's was only a few steps and by the time he had reached High Street his attention was concentrated on the eternal problem of how best to cross the road. For a time it seemed an impossibility, but presently, making a remarkable sortie, he washed himself up on the hospitable steps of the King William. And, yes, he thought, there was time, and ample justification, for a cool and edifying drink before luncheon.

III

His second call could not be paid till the evening, and so after lunch he retired into the garden at the back of the hotel, and submitted his mind to the indoctrination of the press. A large portion of the front page of his paper was devoted to an interview with Vera Bunn-Stephens. Vera, daughter of Sir Harry Bunn-Stephens, had deserted a Belgravia home for a bachelor girl's flat in Battersea, with the intention of leading a fuller life and developing her personality. And now a disgraceful thing had happened. Vera's play about Prince Albert had been withdrawn before the first night on the advice of the police. They had objected, not only to the scene in which the Queen and the Prince give way to the tender passion while listening to Mendelssohn play one of the Prince's own compositions; but also to the whole of Act 2 because of its outspoken treatment of a relationship, hitherto unrecorded, between Mr. Gladstone and Benjamin Disraeli. The picture of Vera Bunn-Stephens showed her smoking a clay pipe in a deep chair with one leg cocked invitingly over the arm. It was all very familiar.

"Vera Bunn-Stephens, a pretty girl in her early twenties . . ." began our special correspondent, and Davie lowered his paper and consulted with an adjacent herbaceous border on that extraordinary journalistic precaution which describes all women as "pretty." George Margin had had his play withdrawn on the ground that the hitherto unrecorded relationship between Mrs. Beeton and Christina Rossetti was unsuitable for public representation, but he had not been described by our special correspondent as "a handsome young man." On the contrary, without comment, patrons of the drama had been allowed to observe him sitting on a packing case, burying a bottle of lager in his beard. It is a rule of journalism, so it appears, that all women up to the age of forty-five must be described as pretty. Is this the last struggle of English gallantry, Davie asked himself: or is it a defense routine insisted on by the editor? A woman who has been described as "pretty" to a million eager readers will surely not claim to have been misrepresented.

Davie turned back from the herbaceous border to the paper: "Vera Bunn-Stephens, a pretty girl in her early twenties," he read, "received me in her bachelor girl flat in Battersea. 'I cannot work with facts,' she explained to me. 'An artist must be free to evaluate the probabilities.'"

Davie lay back in his chair, closed his eyes, and started to evaluate the probabilities about some of his more Rabelaisian acquaintances. All things considered he did not think he would write a play about them. The police, he felt sure . . .

Dr. Davie fell asleep in the sunshine.

Three o'clock, four o'clock. Slowly the shadow of the King William's chimney stack advanced across the lawn. Presently, almost apologetically, it reached the edge of Davie's chair; and he, as though he had felt the summons, stirred in his seat, opened his eyes, quizzed the herbaceous border, and listened to a clink of cups from somewhere further down the garden. It was indeed past four and Alice was serving tea.

Ten minutes later, the chimney shadow on his other side and lengthening now across the lawn, Davie sat in the sun drinking the King William's powerful tea. Beside him on the grass a tray harboured a metal teapot with a handle too hot to hold, a milk jug in which a too adventurous fly had just committed suicide, a plate of thin bread and butter, cress sandwiches, a wedge of sponge cake and some chocolate biscuits. A wasp exchanged a rose's hospitality for the open invitation of a dish of jam. This was tea in the garden as Davie had always known it. He had an affection even for the metal teapot.

For some time he sat there, thinking and watching the advancing shadow of the rest of the hotel, now pursuing its chimney across the green. But when St. Stephen's clock struck five he hauled himself out of his chair and carried in his tray; then walked upstairs to William of Orange's bedroom, washed, brushed his clothes, changed his tie, and zealously attended to his hair. Dr. Davie was going to pay a call on a lady.

At a quarter to six he descended the steps of the King William, took ten paces to the left and stopped before the private door of Madame Jeanne, Hairstyles. The shop, as he had previously ascertained, had shut at five-thirty. A quarter of an hour he reckoned was time enough for Madame Jeanne's tea.

He pressed the electric bell and waited.

IV

"You won't know who I am," began Davie.

But before opening the door Shirley Muffin had had a look at her visitor from behind the pink bows and looped nylon curtain.

"Oh yes, I do," she said. "At least—I don't know your name—but I've seen you call at George's with Inspector Tabor. Is it about Mr. Vanásek?"

"I was hoping to find Miss Jesmond," said Davie. "Do you know if she's in? Or are *you* perhaps Miss Jesmond?"

"No—I'm Miss Muffin," said Shirley, looking a little disappointed. "Miss Jesmond lives on the top floor. It's rather early for her. Will you come up to the lounge. I'll go and see. Who shall I say?"

"Dr. Davie."

Shirley led the way upstairs, settled Davie on an uneasy

140

chair, and proceeded up the next flight calling "Beryl" in a musical kind of voice which Mrs. Coppleston would have commended as entirely suitable to the occasion. But Beryl was not in and "Would you care to wait?" asked Miss Muffin. "She works at Bexminster and she's usually on the ten to six bus."

"Thank you. I'll be grateful."

"I'll tell her as soon as she comes in. Will you excuse me?"

It was not long to wait. A snick of a key was followed by a low whispering in the hall. Then footsteps on the stairs, and the door opened.

"Here is Miss Jesmond," said Shirley.

"How d'you do?" said Davie, and, before Miss Jesmond could go through the tedious business of telling him, he added, "You won't know who I am. I wondered if you'd be so kind as to see me for a few minutes. I—" almost the words stuck in Davie's throat—"I know Mr. Major. I am hoping I may use his name as my introduction."

"Mr. Major is one of my directors," said Miss Jesmond. "I'm sure I shall be very glad to help you if I can. Will you come up to the flat?"

"Thank you. And thank you for your help," Davie said to Miss Muffin.

Miss Jesmond ran up the stairs. "You must excuse my room, Dr. Davie; I've been out all day and I'm sure it's terribly untidy." But that was housewifely precaution. Miss Jesmond's room was neat as a pin, and considerably more comfortable than Miss Muffin's "lounge."

"Please sit down."

Miss Jesmond was not afraid of Dr. Davie. She had spent fifteen years dealing with "the gentlemen," and long ago she had accepted the theory that they were all helpless and that it was her especial purpose in life to succour and assist them.

She was delighted to find yet another gentleman in need of guidance.

She sat down opposite him and said in a voice at once brisk and friendly, "Please tell me what I can do for you."

"I'm sure, Miss Jesmond, that you have heard all about the tragedy at George's," said Davie. "I'm sure you've been asked by the police if you saw anything of a suspicious character on that Saturday, and you will wonder why I should come and ask for your help. It's this—I was a friend of Mr. Vanásek. I am nothing to do with the police—but I am greatly concerned to find, privately, any fact that may not yet have showed itself to be a fact."

"I understand that Mr. Vanásek was killed on Saturday night," said Miss Jesmond. "I was away from Friday evening to Sunday night. So, you see—"

"Yes. I do. I'd hoped you might be able to tell me something. But I see you're not. Please forgive my having bothered you."

"Not at all. I wish I could have helped you."

Davie made as though to rise. It seemed that the interview was over before it had begun. But Miss Jesmond did not move. She sat with her hands folded in her lap, looking down at the carpet.

"The thing that concerns me, Dr. Davie, is the other tragedy, Mr. Coppleston. Do you think—do you think the two things were connected?"

"Yes, Miss Jesmond, I do."

"Mr. Coppleston was a very good man, a very kind man. He was devoted to the firm. It must have been a very wicked person who killed him."

"Did he know any very wicked people?" asked Davie. "Do you?"

Miss Jesmond lifted her head and looked Davie in the

eyes. "I think I must," she said. "But I don't know who they are."

In the silence that followed Davie looked about him. Miss Jesmond had taken trouble with her room. The wallpaper was an aviary of blue and yellow birds perched in a trellis of roses: from the ceiling suspended a Scandinavian lamp-shade: a corner cupboard contained some pretty but not valuable pieces of china: on one side of the room some books stood in a small oak case: on top of the case was a singularly hideous vase. At one end of the mantelshelf stood several spun glass ornaments, a glass bird with a coloured tail, and another, sadly deprived, bereft of his tail in some domestic accident. At the other end there were six paper boats, ranged in procession like a fleet at a royal review.

"Hullo!" said Davie, rising. "Paper boats! I was thinking of paper boats only last night. I'm devoted to paper boats. May I see? Did you make them?"

"No," said Miss Jesmond, and suddenly blushed. "No, I didn't. As a matter of fact it was Mr. Carroll. He always makes a paper boat at board meetings, and I think they're rather sweet, and so I bring them home afterwards."

"Mr. Carroll's particular brand of doodle."

"Yes, in a way. He *does* doodle. They all do. But Mr. Carroll folds his up afterwards and makes a boat."

"I'm an expert on boats," said Davie, picking one up and turning it about on his hand. "What are these pencilled dates? The dates of the meetings?"

"Yes."

"Doodles are a very interesting subject. I remember seeing in the paper once that someone had collected doodles by Churchill and Attlee and Stalin from a conference table somewhere in Russia. I think doodles would make a good learned study. One might publish them with a serious preface on the art, and the significance, of doodling."

Miss Jesmond hesitated, and then, "Well, that's what I do in a way, Dr. Davie. I've got a drawer full of doodles made by my directors. I don't know what they'd say if they knew. Would you like to see some?"

"Very much," said Davie, returning the boat to its position in the fleet.

Miss Jesmond opened a drawer and took out three files, and opened them on the table. "That's Sir Philip—he's always flowers. That's Mr. Major—he's circles. That's Mr. Rowan—he's boxes. They always do the same sort of things. Funny, isn't it?"

Davie leafed through the papers. "I think it's very interesting. One can understand flowers—but why boxes always, why circles? And what about Mr. Caske?"

"I don't think I can show you Mr. Caske," said Miss Jesmond, blushing again. "He's rather awful."

"I mustn't tempt you. The dates at the top of the papers are the dates of the meetings, I suppose?"

"Yes. I added those."

"And these other dates—" began Davie.

"That's just the director's notes," said Miss Jesmond, closing the folders a little abruptly, and carrying them back to their drawer.

"And what does Mr. Carroll draw?"

"Faces—faces of the other directors. Then he makes them into boats."

Davie turned to the mantelshelf and took up another boat and examined the folds. "That's just as I used to make them—still do sometimes. I like them in gold or silver paper. I'll have to give you one of mine, Miss Jesmond."

Miss Jesmond giggled at that, and Davie said goodbye.

"I'm pleased to have met you," said Miss Jesmond.

But after she had shut the door she stood quite still in the middle of the room and bit her finger. The gentleman had been very friendly and nice, but how did she know who he was? Fancy her showing him all those doodles! She must have been crazy—and the last ones with the dates on them. She had always prided herself on her discretion.

It might be shutting the stable door after the horse had gone—but she would have to do it. Miss Jesmond went to the drawer, took out the three files that Davie had seen, and Mr. Caske's, and removed the top sheet from each. Then she took the four bits of paper to the kitchen and burned them in the sink. The flowers, the circles, the boxes: and Mr. Caske's entertaining exercise in the art of tattooing.

Miss Jesmond washed the ashes down the sink, and, as she was about it, filled the kettle. A cup of tea would be comforting. And while the kettle boiled she went into the sitting room and picked up the latest of Mr. Carroll's boats. Very carefully she undid the folds and presently was able to lay the paper on the table. It bore a much creased picture of Mr. Caske. There were no dates. So Miss Jesmond folded it up again and placed it at the head of the fleet, just as the whistling kettle, with an ascending wail, screamed in the kitchen for immediate attention.

V

"If you won't come to the Webern, Dr. Davie, you must have a chocolate," said Miss Bangle. She and Mrs. Mapleton-Morley were just leaving for the evening's festivity.

"A chocolate for Webern: it's a fair exchange. Thank you very much. Have a good time."

"That I faintly doubt," said Miss Bangle. "There's something about Webern . . ."

"There is, indeed."

"I'll tell you all about it later. There's Aunt Maud: I mustn't keep her waiting. Farewell!" And off went Miss Bangle to join Mrs. Mapleton-Morley in the hall.

Davie watched them through the glass door, slowly shutting in its ghostly, leisurely, irritating manner. That door: which one of all those people in the lounge had opened it on Saturday afternoon while Robert Coppleston was telephoning to William Carroll? If only he knew the answer to that, thought Davie, slowly unwrapping his chocolate.

The chocolate had a violet inside, which was very satisfactory. He smoothed out the piece of wrapping on the arm of the chair. It was a particularly splendid bit, part silver, part purple: and it was the right shape for his purpose. Following the practice of years Dr. Davie began to make a boat. Double—fold over that triangle—fold over the other triangle—turn up the bottom bits—bend up the corners . . . he could have done it with his eyes shut.

He placed the silver boat on the coffee table. It was very small, but it was nicely proportioned and the purple bit had come out neatly in the center. Boats didn't always come out nicely proportioned. Sometimes they came out with a blunt centerpiece instead of a neat peak.

To make a good boat your paper must be oblong. If you double a square bit it ends up too wide. It will be the right shape if you then *re-double* it: but that means a smaller boat. Davie felt in his pocket and fished out a letter. A sheet of writing paper, he found, was correctly proportioned. It made a good boat. On another sheet he turned up half an inch. It didn't do so well. With the paper nearer to a square you either got a blunt center, or, by re-doubling, you got a smaller boat.

In his mind's eye Davie reviewed the fleet on Miss Jesmond's mantelshelf. The most recent of the boats had been smaller than the others. But that could hardly have meant that the maker was using a squarer piece of paper. All the doodle papers had been exactly the same size—the normal size of a small writing pad. Presumably William Carroll had doubled and re-doubled his paper to please himself. He had felt like making a small boat. Davie agreed with him: the smaller the boat the more skillful the maker.

It was the end of that rumination, and it would have been the end anyhow, for Joe Major, spying Davie through the glass door, checked his journey to the bar, and entered the lounge to pass the time of night.

"Evening, Dr. Davie, what are you brooding over, all alone?"

"I was pondering on the mysterious fact that everyone has an urge to create. Some people positively make real things. But those that can't do that still have an uncontrollable passion to make something. One chap can't paint a real picture but he likes to add a moustache to the posters on the underground; another can't write a novel but he likes to write a brief anecdote on the wall: and I, who cannot build a boat of wood or iron, can make one out of silver paper. It is an accomplishment in its way, I suppose."

"It certainly is. I wonder what my creative accomplishment is."

"Circles," said Davie, "perfect circles—freehand, as Michelangelo drew them."

"How do you know I draw circles?"

"You drew one last night while we were talking."

"Did I?"

"Yes—and that reminds me. I want to ask an impertinent question."

"Ask on."

"Why, Mr. Major, did you, a man with a mathematical mind, commit the folly of putting back a striking clock?"

"I didn't put the damned thing back," said Joe Major. "Whatever makes you think that?"

"I thought you said you'd adjusted it. You also said it was fast."

"I only said *if* I adjusted it it usually stopped. But not always. Sometimes it doesn't stop. And sometimes it stops of its own sweet obstinate will. If I wasn't fond of it I'd get another. It was given me by an old flame—and I don't like to get rid of it. No—I never touched the thing. She had one of her moods—just like old Jennie used to have. Sometimes she didn't work either."

"You should write your memoirs, Mr. Major."

"I think not, Dr. Davie. I was just on my way to the bar. Will you join me?"

"Thanks very much—but I think I've got to be early tonight."

"Goodnight, then."

"Goodnight."

VI

In the darkness of King Charles's bedroom Davie lay thinking of clocks and boats, boats and clocks.

Boards creaked, and farther down the corridors Festival visitors shut distant doors. Then the house grew silent. Moonlight, shining through thin curtains faintly illuminated the panelled walls. And still Davie lay awake, thinking of clocks and boats.

Joe Major's clock had absolutely nothing to do with the murder of Jiří Vanásek—but because it had stood in a room near to the scene it nagged at Davie's mind. In a vague unreasoning way he felt it *ought* to have had something to do with it. And *did* clocks stop of their own sweet obstinate wills? Perhaps they did—but he couldn't see why they should.

And then from clocks he started thinking about boats, and from boats he proceeded to doodles. Circles, boxes, and flowers—all different: except that on the most recent set there had been one thing common to all three. Common to all three. Common possibly to Mr. Carroll's boat, too, if you could see inside it.

Or wouldn't it be?

Davie almost disturbed his night's rest irretrievably as he asked himself that question—but at the last moment he let it go . . . Or wouldn't it be? It was his last conscious thought; and it was long past midnight.

Wednesday

I

Sitting at breakfast in the Hanoverian bay window of the King William, Dr. Davie was aware of an uncomfortable feeling in the region of his conscience: and not only because he had incontinently partaken of orange juice, puffed wheat, eggs and bacon, and was now engaged in demolishing a rack of toast. Meditating, somewhere between the butter and the marmalade, he had recalled his question of the previous night. "Or wouldn't it be?" And immediately he had been consumed with a desire to do something risky and certainly not honourable. He was not even sure if it could be a fruitful thing to do, but Dr. Davie was a man of quick decisions and he adhered to them obstinately. This morning, somewhere between the first and second piece of toast, he decided that he needed a manicure.

And so, at half past nine, he laid his hand on the latch, and entered the sanctum of Madame Jeanne, not boldly, for truly he found this female reserve not a little alarming with its mysterious engines for the washing and drying and waving of a woman's hair, and, ranged about the walls, all those aids to the beautiful life, the scents, unguents, shampoos, powder boxes, eye shadow, mascara, and those cards of radiating lipsticks, from Cherry Ripe to Lazarus Lilac. Did young women really want to look as though they were dead? It was one of the major mysteries of modern life, Davie was thinking when a bead curtain parted at the back of the salon and Shirley Muffin stepped forward.

"Why, Dr. Davie! This is a surprise," said Miss Muffin. "What can I do for you?"

"Good morning, Miss Muffin," said Davie. "I notice that one of the services you perform is manicure, and I wondered whether you were prepared to engage upon a masculine hand or whether your work is confined to the ladies."

"Oh no—I do have some gentlemen clients. I could take you now as a matter of fact," said Miss Muffin, looking at her engagement book, which was not, as Davie could see, particularly full.

"Thank you—but that's a little too soon. I wonder if you would be free at half past ten," he said, choosing a time which he could see was already allotted to someone else.

"Not ten-thirty I couldn't," said Miss Muffin, meditatively scratching her head with the end of her pencil. "How would eleven o'clock be?"

"It would be all right—and if I should be early I suppose I can go up to the waiting room."

"Yes—where you were yesterday—straight up the stairs—but I won't keep you waiting past your time."

"Thank you," said Davie. "I'll be punctual. Eleven o'clock."

Many a time, sitting in a barber's chair, Davie had wondered about manicurists. For him a haircut involved having his face anointed with a preparation of almonds, simmered

151

beneath a succession of hot towels, stung by an astringent spirit, shocked by cold napkins; and always from these encounters he emerged with a more jaunty step and a brighter eye, and a head perfumed (but only for about twenty minutes) with violet. He loved the whole hedonistic procedure. But never had he consented to have his hands prodded by those attendant maidens who looked so well pleased with themselves and seemed so out of place in that chamber of masculine secrets. Besides, manicure looked painful, and he would have to make some sort of conversation.

But today he had persuaded himself to indulge in this unwelcome extravagance, and so anxious was he to be on time for his appointment that he arrived at Madame Jeanne's a quarter of an hour early, and went quietly upstairs to Miss Muffin's waiting room. No one else was waiting there.

Dr. Davie placed his hat on a chair, as though engaging it for future occupation, and then, leaving the door partly open, he returned to the small landing and peered over the banisters.

There was nothing to see except a romantic picture on the staircase wall, which he remembered from childhood, when it had made the coloured centerpiece of one of those Victorian screens artfully decorated by unmarried daughters with pretty scraps and pictures. (They did not know, these gentle gentlewomen, that they were the *avant-garde* of a movement which would call itself *collage*.)

Sitting at a table in a garden of flowers was a gloomy old gentleman in eighteenth-century clothes. Two white fan-tail pigeons strutted at his feet. In the distance a peacock walked the lawn between immaculate hedges of yew. And, behind the old gentleman, a young man and a beautiful young woman anxiously advanced across the grass—and the woman held a baby in her arms. Surely the old gentleman's determination would not be proof against this? Unfortunately no one was ever to know for certain—but the picture (painted by Ambrose Faddle A.R.A. and exhibited at the Academy in 1882) was entitled "The Reconciliation," and Davie, as a boy, had always taken it for granted that everything was going to be well.

This picture he now noted on the wall of Miss Muffin's staircase, and remembered it and dismissed it, all in the space of two seconds. And then he was mounting the second flight of stairs to the landing which belonged to Miss Jesmond.

Unless suddenly smitten down by illness Miss Jesmond must be out: there could be no doubt of that: but Davie tapped on her sitting room door, and, when he received no answer, he turned the handle (for Miss Jesmond was too much at home with Miss Muffin to need locks and keys, and Mrs. Friske had to get in with dustpan and brush on Wednesdays), entered Miss Jesmond's room, shut the door behind him, and went straight across to the fireplace.

Picking up the smallest of the boats, the one on which Miss Jesmond had pencilled last Friday's date, he unfolded it with quick practiced fingers. And there was the much creased drawing of Daniel Caske: and not a bad likeness either.

The paper differed from the doodles of the other directors in two respects. The answer to "Or wouldn't it be?" was no. There was no date on the paper. And the paper was certainly squarer: which accounted for the smaller boat. Someone at some time had sliced a bit off Mr. Carroll's paper. And someone, thought Davie, had sent that bit of paper in an envelope to Jiří Vanásek. If Mr. Carroll had made his paper into a boat, had someone subsequently remade it into a

smaller boat? And had he—Davie—made an important discovery? Or was he making a grotesque assumption? For the
moment he did not argue the probabilities. He merely noted
them.

Davie carefully refolded the boat, replaced it at the head
of the fleet, and crossed to the door; and there with his fist
on the handle, he suddenly stopped. Someone—it couldn't
be Miss Jesmond—but someone was labouring up the stairs
with deep grampus breathing.

There were three doors on the landing—one opening presumably on Miss Jesmond's bedroom, and one, the one
facing the head of the stairs, probably opening on the
kitchen.

The heavy steps, which had now reached the landing,
went past the sitting room door, and ended somewhere to
the left, in the kitchen, if it were the kitchen.

Davie opened the door with great caution and peeped
out.

The kitchen door was half open. Behind glass panels he
could see the shadow of a vast body, moving its arms as if
getting ready for business—tying on an apron perhaps. And
it was singing in a deep gritty contralto voice.

> How can I live without you?
> How can I let you go?

The inquiry was stilled for a moment as the singer planked a
bucket in the sink and turned on a tap that juddered hideously for lack of a new washer.

"Drat the thing," said the singer—"You that I worship so,
dear—"

Taking advantage of the clatter, Davie shut the door,
tiptoed to the head of the stairs, and descended them as fast
as he dared. But as he reached the half-landing, uncom-

154

fortably aware that the voice of devotion had become louder, he glanced up and caught a fleeting impression of a great red face staring at him over the banisters. "You that I worship—hey! What do *you* want?" it said.

Davie treated the question as rhetorical. Remembering the difficulty that the voice had had in ascending, he did not expect to be followed. Nipping into the waiting room, he grabbed his hat, ran on down the stairs past "The Reconciliation," and came to halt outside Madame Jeanne's salon. Then, quickly adjusting his manners, he opened the door, and, "There you are, Dr. Davie," said Miss Muffin. "You're right on time. Will you sit here?"

"Thank you," said Davie. He wished he hadn't been such a fool. To look up, to show himself to the red-faced voice, that was idiotic. If he got into trouble it would serve him right. It was none of his business to snoop round Miss Jesmond's room. Yes—but he had known that before he did it.

"Now—if you will put your hand on the table, Dr. Davie—" said Miss Muffin.

As he had suspected, manicure was vaguely painful, vaguely unpleasant, and, to him, faintly improper.

As he had also suspected, it involved conversation.

"It was ever such a shock to me," said Miss Muffin, "when Inspector Tabor came to see me on Monday. I didn't know then what had happened at George's. To think that I may have seen the murderer."

"Did you?" said Davie, speaking as easily as he could. "How was that?"

"Well, I was late that night. It was Saturday and I had had a friend with me, watching the television. After my friend had gone I went downstairs to make a cup of tea, and there were things to do—you know—"

"Yes, I do."

"Tidying and so on—and then, as I was going upstairs to bed, I remembered I hadn't switched the telly off, and so I went into the lounge and did that, and then I went over to the window and looked out, and there was a man coming out of George's. Of course I thought it was Mr. Vanásek, because he did go out for late walks—but I suppose it wasn't."

"And where did the man go?"

"Down the alley beside George's."

"I suppose you've told Inspector Tabor all this."

"Oh yes—and he wrote it all down."

And then Davie asked the question that mattered most.

"What time was this? Do you know?"

"Yes—I do exactly, as a matter of fact, because I looked at the clock in the kitchen and I said to myself, Goodness! I didn't know it was that late, I said—and that was just before I came upstairs. It must have been two minutes past twelve when I saw him."

"*Two minutes past twelve,*" said Davie to his heart. "Dear God! It fits, it fits like a glove."

"Dr. Davie!" said Miss Muffin. "You are naughty. I shall never do these cuticles if you don't keep still."

"I'm sorry. I'm a great fidget," said Davie. "You didn't see this man again? If it had been Mr. Vanásek he'd have come back."

"No I didn't. I went to bed at once."

"And you didn't see anyone else go to the shop?"

"Not till Monday early. Mrs. Bazeley called at about a quarter to nine—but the shop wasn't open and she went down the alley. I expect she was going to the back door."

"Anyone else?"

"There was a man went down the alley at about nine. He might have been to Mr. Vanásek's. He came back about two minutes later."

"Was the man anything like the man you saw on Saturday night?"

"I couldn't say—really I couldn't say. I wasn't looking properly."

Davie had visited Madame Jeanne in order to take a look at Miss Jesmond's boat. It was not the boat that excited him now. The false clue, he was thinking. *The Motor* masquerading in the covers of *Punch*. It was possible. Certainly it was. He looked at the man in the glass who was having his nails polished by Shirley Muffin, and he saw that his eyes were bright with excitement. But there's no point in telling Tabor that a man left George's at two minutes past twelve, he was thinking. He knows that. And I can't tell him who I think it was: I've no proof. And I'm certainly not going to admit to rummaging about in Miss Jesmond's room—even though the two bits of paper almost certainly fit. Joining them up won't show who put them apart, and that's what matters.

"There we are," said Miss Muffin. "You don't often have a manicure, do you, Dr. Davie? I can tell that because you're so fidgety."

II

Davie had received his warning on Tuesday that the inquests would be held this Wednesday afternoon. The coroner was free, the pathologist had not encountered any mysteries. The sooner, therefore, the better.

As he expected, it was a formal affair. Inspector Tabor and he gave evidence about the finding of Jiří Vanásek, and William Carroll and Mr. Dew of the finding of Robert Coppleston. The county pathologist gave evidence about the immediate cause of death. There was nothing complicated about

157

that. Both men had been violently bashed on a vital spot in the throat.

The coroner then postponed the proceedings for further investigation.

Nothing had been uncovered, but for Davie the inquest marked an end to his retirement. On Monday and Tuesday he had not felt he could engage in festivities, hadn't felt like going out even to so sober an entertainment as an organ recital at St. Stephen's. But this evening, sitting in the lounge at the King William before dinner, Mildred Meade-Fuller had persuaded him to go to the program of "Jazz and Poetry" at the Market Hall.

"My dear," she had said, "I think you ought to go. I do indeed. You needn't feel disrespectful. It's not as though you were likely to enjoy it."

"I daresay you're right, Mildred."

"Of course I am, R.V. You don't want to seek trouble."

"Nonsense, Mildred. We can't escape it. Man is born to trouble as the sparks fly upwards."

"What's that, R.V.?"

"I was only quoting an example of Lord Snow's favourite law of thermodynamics."

"You can't do that here, R.V. You're not in Cambridge now. Do say you'll come."

"All right, Mildred. I am, I admit, considerably intrigued. Does the jazz enhance the poetry, or the poetry enhance the jazz? Does it happen separately or all at once?"

"My dear, that is what we are going to find out. It's all too exciting. I do think we ought to support the *avant-garde*."

"*Avant-garde* of what, Mildred? That's the point."

The organizers of the King's Lacy Festival had certainly picked a winner with "Jazz and Poetry." The Market Hall had been sold out for the first time in living memory, for, besides a fair number of Festival visitors, the youth of King's Lacy (who wouldn't have been seen dead at the opera or the string quartets) had been attracted by the word jazz, by the band, which was a good one, and by the name of Persephone Popondopoulos, who, though born and brought up in Penge, was of Greek descent, and looked like something out of *The Odyssey*.

The ground floor of the Market Hall, not having originally been intended as a place of entertainment, was not raked, and Davie was sitting in the front row of the gallery. It is a considerable bore to pay a guinea for the back view of a lot of other people's heads. Far better to look down on them like a god.

While he waited he amused himself spotting faces. None of the distinguished old ladies had risked it. There was no Lady Cranberry, no Miss Myrtle, no Mrs. Mapleton-Morley. But Sir Philip and Lady Gossamer were there, sitting in the second row, and at the end of the same row Davie noticed the sandy-haired Mr. Rowan. He had a woman with him and an excited little girl: wife and daughter probably. He didn't see the other chap—Caske: nor Mr. Major, which was not surprising. He did see Miss Muffin. She was sitting with a rosy young man: perhaps he was the friend who had come to watch the telly on Saturday, and had kept Miss Muffin up so conveniently late.

And that was as much quizzing as he had time for. They were off.

It was not a concert of pop music. Here were jazz symphonies and serious poems set to jazz rhythms. And why not, Davie found himself thinking after Persephone Popondopoulos had brought the house down by singing two jazzed up versions of Elizabeth Barrett Browning. Why not? It was Homer, not some Hollywood comedian, who had written

"Smiling through tears." It was Ibsen, not Noel Coward, who first heard the younger generation knocking on his door. If this was what the jazz musicians could do to poetry he was all for it. The only question—the eternal question of criticism—was, is it well done? By the time Persephone Popondopoulos had sung "Tears, Idle Tears," with a heart-piercing exposition of the theme on a solo trumpet, Davie had surrendered completely.

And now the musicians took a rest and the first of the poets who were to read their own works appeared. This was George Canackers and he brought with him a distinguished Yugoslav whose name was not known at all to the citizens of King's Lacy. But George Canackers, who had spent a considerable time in the dressing room making himself suitably untidy, explained how distinguished the Yugoslav poet was, and for five minutes the audience listened in a stunned silence as the author read his poems in the original tongue. After which George Canackers read his own translation of the poems for the benefit of those members of the audience who were unfamiliar with Slavonic. George Canackers was indeed unfamiliar with Slavonic himself, and had prepared his versions from a literal translation provided by an intermediary: which made no difficulties for George Canackers, who had made a brilliant translation of Camoëns without knowing a word of Portuguese and was currently engaged on some brilliant translations from the Chinese. It was an understood thing that George Canackers was brilliant. His publishers said so. And George Canackers had never denied it. It was a pity that he was such a bad reader.

Five minutes later the return of Miss Popondopoulos was greeted with the enthusiasm of intense relief. She ended the first part of the program with a lyric by a contemporary poet, singing against a recording of herself singing against a recording of herself singing against a recording of herself, thereby creating a work in four parts for one voice. At one point Miss Popondopoulos sang into the bell of a trumpet. At another she placed her head inside the grand piano. She also sang roguishly through the strings of the harp.

The youth of King's Lacy was enchanted. And so indeed was Dr. Davie. He adored magic.

The second part of the program proceeded in the same happy mood with the band playing "Mini-skirt Blues"; harmless Antony Waste reading his perfectly intelligible poems; Milly Mannering singing songs to a guitar ("Tarnish my reputation, someone," "Lie down strike," and "Near normal temperature"); the band again with "Elegy for a Missed Appointment."

And then George Canackers returned to the platform, and prefaced a reading of his poems by the unexpected announcement that he was dedicating his performance to the gallant fighters for democracy in the Chinese Republic—but whether that implied a spiritual and poetic donation or whether Mr. Canackers intended positively to contribute his fee to the cause was not apparent, though it was generally understood that he considered his poetry a sufficient offering in itself.

But if anyone in the audience supposed he was now to hear uplifting verses about Peace and the Brotherhood of Man and the Mission of the Proletariat, he was swiftly disenchanted, for George Canackers proceeded to read a long sexy poem to which a supposed strength had been given by the inclusion and repetition of a number of four-letter words.

At the conclusion George Canackers would have been happy if the audience had cheered, delighted if some had booed. But the audience did neither. The fact was that some had not heard; some had been unable to believe their

ears; and a gentle few had not understood. Miss Mainte-
nance, who was reporting the concert for *The King's Lacy
Echo,* and was one of those who had mistaken the drift,
afterwards informed her readers that "Mr. Canackers
charmed his auditory with his subtle imagery": which an-
noyed Mr. Canackers very much when he received it three
weeks later from four press cutting agencies.

The atmosphere in the Market Hall as Mr. Canackers retired was cold: the minds of his "auditory" full of doubt.

It needed Persephone Popondopoulos to restore the temperature—which she did immediately by appearing in a
long tight frock of silver tissue to sing with the band "The
Dustbin Song" by the well-known contemporary poet Stephen Mossop, followed by a jazzed up version of "Break,
Break, Break," which brought the fans to their feet in an awe-
inspiring demonstration of approval which reached its apex
as the conductor whisked an enormous trick bouquet out of
the bass tuba and presented it to Miss Popondopoulos on his
knees.

"My goodness!" said Davie to Mildred Meade-Fuller as
they struggled out onto the pavement, "I haven't enjoyed
anything so much for years."

"Including Mr. Canackers, R.V.?"

"Well—no, Mildred."

"It *can't* be *avant-garde* to use those old-fashioned
words, can it, R.V.?"

Davie laughed aloud.

"You have a point there, Mildred. But the rest of it— What
professionalism!"

III

Alec Rowan steered the car into the garage of No. 12
Philpot Way. Maureen and Sonia climbed out.

"We'll go on, Alec," said Maureen. "Come along, Sonia; it's long past your bedtime."

"I must say goodnight to the gnomes," said Sonia.

"The gnomes are telling each other anecdotes," said Alec. "Run along in."

"Oh *Daddy!* What's anecdotes, Mummy?"

"Just stories," said Maureen as she and Sonia walked along the brick path between the house and the herbaceous border.

"But why—"

The telephone was ringing as they opened the door.

"Answer it, Sonia—quick!" said Maureen, and Sonia, running forward, slipped on the parquet and fell down. By the time Maureen had picked her up the bell had stopped.

"Oh God! Howling as usual," said Alec in the doorway. "Who was that calling?"

"We weren't in time."

"It only began as you opened the door."

"I know—but Sonia fell down."

"I'm only a little girl," said Sonia in a detestable phrase she had caught from her mother.

"Don't talk that dreary rubbish, Sonia," said Alec, but not crossly. "We know how old you are, *and* how many hands you've got."

"Alec!"

"I'm only asking her not to whine. It's terribly boring, and the best children don't do it."

"Alec—I do wish—there, there, never mind darling, you're tired."

"I'm *not* tired," wailed Sonia, and so, attended by her mother, stumped upstairs, howling.

It was too often this way in the Rowan household. Alec was right and hard: Maureen was wrong and weak. Sonia found weakness best suited to her conveniences. She howled at will.

Alec mixed himself a whisky and water and took it down the passage to the study. He disliked missing telephone calls. At that time of night it wouldn't have been one of Maureen's gossips. It might have been important.

IV

Miss Jesmond had travelled home on her usual bus that evening, and at five minutes to six had let herself in at the front door and climbed the two flights of stairs to her flat. First she went to her bedroom and changed her shoes and washed her face and hands, and fluffed out her hair in front of the looking glass. Then she went to her open window, and looked down on the garden of the King William, now in green shadow except at the end of the lawn, which still shone brightly in the sun. Beyond the garden wall stretched old, irregular, red roofs. A few fine trees marked the gardens of larger houses. Miss Jesmond loved her "view." When she had satisfied herself that it was all there, and when she had taken another look at the two or three persons still lingering in the King William garden, she went into the kitchen and prepared supper.

Miss Jesmond did not believe in living on boiled eggs and bits of cheese as so many people do when left alone. She was a good cook and she did herself modestly well. Tonight she had brought home a slice of halibut (that noble and expensive fish) and the way to cook it, in Miss Jesmond's opinion, was in the oven. So first she lit it and placed the regulator at mark 4. Then she set a saucepan of water to boil. Then she took a piece of silver foil and buttered it. On this she laid pepper and salt, a few chopped herbs, and a bay leaf. Then she sat the halibut on the bay leaf, put another bay leaf on top and wrapped up the fish in a silver buttery parcel, ready to pop into the oven on a fireproof dish: but not before she had shelled the peas: the two must be ready together. At that thinness she thought fifteen minutes would do for the halibut. Afterwards there would be raspberries and cream.

What with one thing and another it was not till half past six that Miss Jesmond went into the sitting room, intending to lie back in the armchair and smoke a cigarette while she scanned *The Bexminster Weekly Star*, which came out on Wednesdays, and was always a considerable source of entertainment. She enjoyed reading about the rows at the Bexminster council meetings: someone was always in a state of indignation about something. And then there were the reports of all the Bexminster societies, the bazaars, the flower shows, the amateur theatricals. This week it was the operatic society's summer production of *The Mikado*. Miss Jesmond had got as far as "Miss Muriel Smith sang charmingly as Yum-Yum, while the other two little maids from school were in the capable hands of the Misses Gladys Ewart, and Daphne Jones," when a fluttering of wings on the windowsill caused her to look up—and it was only then that she saw the note on the table.

Mrs. Friske, thought Miss Jesmond, getting up and crossing to the table in the window. Mrs. Friske was a great note writer. Usually she left messages like, "dear Miss J you need some more washing powder Mrs. Friske"; or "dear Miss J I am sorry I broke the vegetable dish Mrs. Friske." This note was longer.

"dear Miss J I ought to tell you there was a man this morning just when I come. I did not meet him going up but when I look over the ballisters there he was going down so I think he must have been up and slip down when I was in the kitchen. I do not see anything wrong but you better look his hair was grey but I did not see his face proper Mrs. Friske."

Several times at the office that day Miss Jesmond had found her thoughts wandering to the elderly gentleman who had called on her on the previous evening. She felt she had been too easily impressed by his urbane ("urbane" was not one of Miss Jesmond's words, but that was what she had in mind) manners. And then, when she had passed Mr. Major in one of the corridors and had said "I met a friends of yours last night, Mr. Major—Dr. Davie," he had looked for a moment as though he didn't recollect the name. It had made her uncomfortable all day—and now here was this note from Mrs. Friske.

As Miss Jesmond stood there, twisting the paper in her fingers, she remembered the halibut and the peas, and hastened into the kitchen. And only just in time. She put the fish on a plate and poured the melted butter over it from the silver wrapping—a natural herb-flavored sauce. Then she put the peas in a dish—an unnecessary refinement, but Miss Jesmond liked everything to be just so—took a napkin out of a drawer, and settled herself down at the small table in the kitchen. But with every mouthful her thoughts were with the grey-haired man who had climbed her stairs that morning. Was he Dr. Davie? She had no right to assume it, but she could not dismiss the idea from her mind. And, whoever he was, this grey-haired man, what had he wanted?

Miss Jesmond rose from the table and went into her bedroom. Everything looked as usual. She opened one or two drawers: such treasures as she had were in their usual places. She crossed the landing and went into the sitting room. Her first thought was the doodle drawer. Nothing had been disturbed. She turned to the fireplace, and immediately something attracted her attention. The leading boat was facing the wrong way. She had pencilled a date on each boat, but that side was always turned towards the wall. The leading boat, the little boat, the one she had unfolded on the previous night, was showing its date. She *knew*, she knew for an absolute certainty that she had put it back the other way round. Someone had been in the room—someone besides Mrs. Friske, for Mrs. Friske had been strictly enjoined never to dust the mantelshelf, from that fatal day when Miss Jesmond had come home to find a note on the table: "dear Miss J one of the glass birds tails has come off Mrs. Friske."

Someone else had been in the room, and picked the boat up, and had perhaps unfolded it. There was no damage to property in that—but *why* had anyone wanted to look at it?

Miss Jesmond ran down the stairs and knocked at Miss Muffin's door.

"Shirley! Can I come in?"

The door was opened by Shirley's young man.

"Beryl—you know Jack Crumble, don't you? We're just going to the 'Jazz and Poetry' at the Market Hall."

"Have you one minute, Shirley?"

"Just one, Beryl. What is it?" And then as she saw that Beryl was making unmistakable gestures with her eyebrows in the direction of Mr. Crumble, she added, "Come into the bedroom."

"Thanks."

"What's up, Beryl?" said Shirley when she had shut the door.

"Promise not to ask questions."

"All right."

"I want to know if you have seen that Dr. Davie today."

"Yes—I have. He came for a manicure."

"I knew it," said Miss Jesmond. "What time?"

"He came in about half past nine and made an appoint-

167

ment for eleven. And he kept it on the dot. Whatever's the matter, Beryl?"

Shirley had been told not to ask questions—but she did: and Beryl had not intended to answer any—but she did.

"Mrs. Friske saw a man like him on my staircase when she came today—and that's at eleven o'clock or a little earlier. I just wondered—"

"It couldn't have been Dr. Davie, Beryl."

"I daresay not—but it was someone and I don't like it."

"I don't like it either—but he's not there now. I shouldn't worry. You haven't lost anything, have you?"

"No."

"Perhaps Dr. Davie went to the waiting room and lost his way."

"I suppose he could have done that."

"I must go, Beryl, or we'll miss the show. I'm sorry about this—but don't worry."

But Beryl did worry. When she got upstairs she unfolded the little boat and examined it carefully. She *couldn't* see why anyone should be interested in it. So she folded it up and put it back in its place. She was not going to panic. She would keep her boat.

Then she remembered she had not had her raspberries and cream. So she sat down again and finished her supper and afterwards she did the washing up. Then she went downstairs and through Miss Muffin's rooms into the Beauty Parlour. And there she telephoned to 12 Philpot Way. There was no answer. She tried again at half past nine. There was no answer. Mr. Rowan, Maureen, and Sonia were at "Jazz and Poetry" at the Market Hall, two hundred yards up the street.

After Shirley had come home Miss Jesmond slipped out to a telephone booth and tried again at half past ten. There was no answer. That was when Sonia was lying on the floor howling, and Alec Rowan was standing in the doorway saying "Who was that calling?"

Miss Jesmond went home to bed. Perhaps she had worked herself up about it too much. But she meant to speak to Mr. Rowan in the morning.

Not many yards away from Miss Jesmond's room, as the bat flies, the not wholly commendable Dr. Davie was thinking to himself as he snipped out the light in Judge Jeffreys's bedchamber, "The agent in this matter is like Mr. Canackers, remarkably like him. He is 'brilliant.' He is successful. And he's a fraud. One sees through Mr. Canackers because he will put himself in the spotlight. But the chap we have to deal with is so cool, and so reserved, that we don't get the opportunity to look at him. I think he is exactly the reverse of what he appears to be. If I am right. If I am right."

Thursday

I

MRS. BAZELEY'S INDISPOSITION ON MONDAY MORNING HAD NOT been due entirely to a temporary failure of her vital mechanism. She had been shocked, certainly, to be told of Jiří Vanásek's death—and so soon after having visited the shop. But what had shocked her more than that was the manner of telling. Mrs. Bazeley hated the police: she did not want them in her shop: and on that day least of all did she want them. She had been gravely disturbed when Inspector Tabor introduced himself—and almost relieved when she heard the reason for his visit. For half a minute she had been afraid he was going to accuse her of something or other. She had nothing to tell them about Jiří Vanásek, and her momentary fit of dizziness assisted their departure.

That afternoon Mrs. Bazeley had kept very much to herself. She had not gone out at all on Tuesday, and it was only as a result of Tommy's importunity that she had made a foray early on Wednesday morning.

But now, on Thursday morning, Mrs. Bazeley was beginning to feel herself again. She had made various profitable sales on Wednesday afternoon, including the new Staffordshire figures, and several pieces of jewellery. And one knowledgeable collector had treated with her over an oval Queen Anne looking glass. She did not mind that. Mrs. Bazeley admired an expert and took an oriental pleasure in striking a bargain. She had sold the glass, that was the great thing, and the exercise had done her a power of good.

On Thursday morning at about half past nine Mrs. Bazeley opened her back door. At that time of day the sun was on the front of the house and most of the garden was in shadow. But the flower bed at the end of the garden had caught the light and Mrs. Bazeley went up the path to have a look at it. Tommy watched her from the doorstep and turned back. In his opinion it was much too early for that sort of thing. The shop window, now—at this time of the morning that offered an entirely different prospect: there was a particularly good place in the sun between the jewellery and the Rockingham teapot. Thither Tommy bent his steps, and had been happily established there for some three minutes when the door opened with an hysterical tinkle. A customer entered the shop.

"Hullo," said Dr. Davie.

Tommy opened one eye and shut it again. Davie bent down and stroked Tommy's head. "You are a very fine cat," he said. "A very fine cat indeed. I doubt if I've ever seen a finer cat."

Tommy started to purr.

"Look out for the Rockingham," Davie added, as Tommy rolled over on his back. Tommy gave a loud sigh, as who might say, "To hell with the Rockingham! I want my middle stroked." Davie stroked it, and then straightened himself and started to look around the shop. No one had answered the bell. That was because Mrs. Bazeley, at the top of the garden, had not heard it.

Mrs. Bazeley's shop was not large but it contained some beautiful things. Davie was amused by a Chinese teapot, late eighteenth century, made for the English market. It was unmistakably Chinese, but the decorations bore flowers of an English sort. Near it was an English sugar bowl—and that bore a splendid imitation of the Chinese willow pattern.

In the far corner of the shop was a small corner cupboard with curved doors. Davie had long wanted one of these. It was just the thing for his college rooms. He crossed the shop and opened the cupboard door to inspect the inside; and as he did so Mrs. Bazeley entered the shop behind him.

"Ah—good morning, Mrs. Bazeley," Davie said, turning about. "I came in to look at your lovely things. I hope you remember me. I've got several things from you in the past."

"I remember you," said Mrs. Bazeley. "You are Dr. Davie —but you ought not to be looking in my cupboards."

"I'm very sorry—but I assumed everything in the shop was for sale."

"Not that. That cupboard is private."

"I'm sorry. It didn't say so."

For a few seconds they looked at each other. Then Davie said, "It's no use my pretending that I haven't seen what's inside it. May I ask where you got that very beautiful Europa and the Bull?"

"I bought it," said Mrs. Bazeley. "At an auction. A recent auction."

"The Massingham auction?" asked Davie. "On Friday last?"

"Yes."

"But it was Jiří Vanásek who bought that. How does it come to be here?"

"I don't know why I should have to answer all these questions."

"You don't have to answer them."

Mrs. Bazeley shrugged her shoulders. "The Europa is here for a very simple reason. Mr. Vanásek bought it on my behalf. I was unable to go to the auction. He brought it back on Friday, and I collected it from him on Saturday afternoon, after we'd both closed."

Davie stared at her.

"But that's not true, Mrs. Bazeley."

"Not true!"

"I was with Mr. Vanásek on Saturday night. I didn't leave him till half past eleven. The Europa was there then."

"You saw him on Saturday night?"

"I did."

For some seconds Mrs. Bazeley did not speak. She stared at the middle button of Davie's jacket, and her fingers fiddled with the ends of the mauve scarf which lay triangularly across her shoulders.

Presently she said, "All right—if you must know—it wasn't Saturday afternoon. I went in early on Monday morning—and took it. I saw Mr. Vanásek on the floor. I saw he was dead. So I took it and wrapped it in a silk handkerchief I found, and put it in my bag and came out again as quickly as I could."

"*That* silk handkerchief?" asked Davie, pointing to a folded square which lay on the shelf beside the Europa.

"Yes."

"You've put yourself in a madly awkward position, Mrs. Bazeley. I don't suppose you had anything to do with this tragedy—"

"Of course not—and don't talk to me as if you were a policeman."

"The fact remains that the police are hunting for the Europa as a possible clue to the murder. If you don't tell them you have it, you are concealing evidence. If you do tell them you are admitting that you stole it."

"Stole it!"

"I think so. Jiří Vanásek talked to me about the Europa. He did not say that he had bought it on commission. Indeed he rather indicated that he'd never bring himself to part with it. This silk handkerchief too—don't you understand that that also may be evidence?"

"Why should it be?"

"Where was it?"

"In Mr. Vanásek's pocket."

"It wasn't in Mr. Vanásek's pocket when I saw him last thing on Saturday night."

"Mr. Vanásek always carried a handkerchief in his outside pocket. It was part of him."

"I know that—but it wasn't that one."

"I don't see how you can know that."

"Can you swear that this handkerchief was in Mr. Vanásek's pocket?"

Mrs. Bazeley lowered her eyelids. That morning she had coloured them pale blue. It made her look strangely like a dead pheasant.

"Well—no—it wasn't. I wasn't thinking. It was in his hand."

"*In his hand!* The fingers must have been rigid."

"It was only just caught in his hand. It came away with a tweak."

"*You took it from his hand.*" Davie whispered the words incredulously.

"I had to have something," said Mrs. Bazeley coolly. "And I wasn't going to stay any longer than necessary."

"Why on earth did you take the Europa?"

"I wanted it. I wanted it more than I ever wanted anything. I knew he'd only just got it. I knew it hadn't been offered for sale. I thought no one had seen it. I thought no one would know. I wanted it. Why shouldn't I have it? He had no wife, no children. What will happen to his things? I shall say that he bought it for me—as my agent."

"Can you prove that?"

"Can you disprove it?"

"I expect the bank could."

"The Europa is *mine*, I tell you. *Mine*. I only went to collect what was my own."

"Will you go to the police or shall I?"

"I'm not going."

"Will you give me that handkerchief?"

"Yes."

"You're sure you won't go to the police?"

"I will not."

"You must expect them to come to you then," said Davie, and as Mrs. Bazeley made no further remark he said, "I'm sorry about this," turned, and walked out of the shop.

As he shut the door the hysterical bell roused Tommy from his slumber. He was not troubled. He had just remembered a clump of cat-mint which made very good sitting at this time of the morning. Mrs. Bazeley had often shooed him off it, but Tommy took no notice of that. "I never heard such nonsense," he used to reason. "If a cat can't sit on the cat-mint who can?"

Davie went on down the street to the police station. In Mrs. Bazeley's shop he had been reminded of something which justified his speculations. His other ideas had been hunches, guesses. This new thought pinned them all together. He was ready now to ask Inspector Tabor to listen to him.

II

The King's Lacy Festival always ended with a particularly agreeable function. On the Thursday evening there was a buffet supper at Lacy Hall followed by madrigals sung on a barge tethered under the Palladian bridge that spans the small lake like the waist of an hourglass. If it rained the party could always be transferred to the house. If it were fine the company stood on the bridge and beside the lake. It was a splendid occasion. Lights shone around the water, not strings of lights like those on a seaside promenade, but lights among the water lilies and among the far rushes; lights on the island, lights among the trees, and lights beside that grass paved walk which rises to the lovely little temple of Apollo erected in 1762 by Rachel, Lady Gossamer.

So far from being a votary of the ancient gods, Lady Gossamer had been an earnest evangelical dissenter, and had lavished a deal of money all over the county in building what were known as Lady Gossamer chapels. But she had also been a woman of taste and discernment, and where she thought a vista required a temple in the classical tradition, she erected it with as much enthusiasm as she brought to the building of a chapel for the uses of her own sterner theology. Most of the Lady Gossamer chapels have been pulled down long ago to make way for cinemas and garages and supermarkets. But the temple of Apollo in the park at Lacy remains, and claims a tribute to a noble woman.

The Thursday night party had become a famous event. It was customary to invite the opera cast and any other of the Festival artists who could be present, and that made an added attraction to a gala occasion. People liked to have a squint at the nobs, at Anatole Bysshe, the music director, at Mrs. Manifold, the producer; and many people this year were hoping to get more than a squint at George Commice and John Jessop, the spectacular stars of the opera: it would be interesting to see what they looked like with their clothes on.

Even people not amiably concerned with the Festival liked to come to this final entertainment. Daniel Caske never attended anything else, but he always brought Amy to this. She particularly enjoyed the grand ascent of rockets at the end, cannonading their coloured stars over the water, to the considerable astonishment of the residents, who squawked their disapproval from shadowy margins of the lake. "Poor things!" Amy always used to say.

By some miraculous dispensation it had never rained yet at the Thursday party. But on this Thursday the clouds had begun to gather soon after lunch time. It was not surprising. There had been a solid week of spectacularly beautiful weather. It had to break some time: the radio report said it would break that night: the question was—would it hold till half past ten.

At seven o'clock the Festival committee considered the matter.

"We eat at half past eight and you sing at nine-thirty," said Lady Gossamer. "What do you say, Anatole?"

Anatole Bysshe looked at the sky.

"We wait," he said. "At quarter past nine we either walk down to the barge or we walk into the salon. Don't despair of the barge, but have the chairs ready."

Mrs. Manifold said, "I think we shall just make it."

"That's very brave," said Lady Gossamer, "but people will be cross if they get wet."

"We can transfer to the house at any point in the program. It's not a difficult operation. We aren't dealing with scenery and costumes."

"But we are dealing with a lot of old ladies."

"We've never missed yet," pleaded Mrs. Manifold. "I'd be very sorry to break our run."

"So would I," said Philip Gossamer. "Let's assume it's on until we can see it isn't."

At nine o'clock they met again on the terrace.

"It's inky," said Lady Gossamer, almost with a note of triumph in her voice. Violet Gossamer was ever the first to predict disaster. "Of course we must have it in the salon."

"But the clouds are high," said Mrs. Manifold. "That's always a good sign."

"My opinion is worthless," said Anatole Bysshe. "I've rehearsed that first piece as I've never rehearsed anything. I want to do it."

"So do I," said Mrs. Manifold. "Do let's take a risk."

"It's going to rain," said Lady Gossamer.

"Yes—but not absolutely at once," said Sir Philip. "I think we'll do it—but we must be punctual to the dot."

"Bless your heart," said Mrs. Manifold. "I'll go and tell Albert. We'll give the warning five minutes early."

"You'll regret this," said Lady Gossamer. "Don't say I didn't warn you."

"Dearest Violet!" said Anatole Bysshe. "If we listened to all your warnings—"

And so, a few minutes later, at the foot of the great staircase Albert beat upon the gong, and "Ladies and gentlemen," he proclaimed, "will you please proceed to the lake. The performance will begin in fifteen minutes precisely."

Davie had been standing in a corner, eating the salmon mayonnaise and strawberries and cream traditional to the occasion, and watching the company. He had become interested in the five directors of Bexminster Electronics. Mr. Major was not present. That was to be expected. Nor, so far as he could see, was Mr. Carroll. That was unexpected, and to Davie reassuring. Philip Gossamer, an indefatigable host, had been moving among the company continually, but had recently walked out onto the terrace with Mrs. Manifold. Mr. Caske, with a rather dreary female, was standing with Mr. Rowan, who was accompanied by the same woman as on the previous evening, and the same child. The two women were talking. Slightly apart, Rowan and Caske were standing heads together in close conference.

"Hallo, Dr. Davie!"

It was Miss Bangle, resplendent in an emerald feather boa, magnificent against the auburn hair and eminently unsuitable for a probably wet evening.

"I'm on my own."

"That's unusual."

"Aunt Maud wouldn't come. She said it was bound to rain. Will it?"

"They've just been out on the terrace attempting to discover," said Davie.

It was at that moment that Albert smote upon his gong, drawing all eyes to himself as he made his proclamation. Davie looked that way with everyone else, and suddenly was glad to be standing near the door. In the middle of the throng, midway between himself and Albert, he had perceived Miss Jesmond.

As a tribute no doubt to the place and the occasion she was wearing a green linen coat and skirt and a hat like half a grapefruit, stuffed with lilies of the valley. All which he uselessly noted while his mind was asking why she should be there. Miss Jesmond was not at all the kind of person to squander two guineas on this sort of lark. Certainly she was the last person he wanted to meet.

"Let's lead on," said Davie to Miss Bangle. "First come get the best places on the bridge."

III

The music began with a masterly contrivance dreamed up by Mrs. Manifold and magnificently realized by Anatole Bysshe. With a discreetly scattered audience there was no great murmur to subdue, and such talking as there was was instantly hushed as the company heard the distant music of two horns coming from the far end of the lake.

Presently the voices under the bridge replied:

> How sweet the answer Echo makes
>   To Music at night,
> When, rous'd by lute or horn, she wakes,
> And, far away, o'er lawns and lakes,
>   Goes answering light.

It was Tom Moore arranged by Anatole Bysshe, and never were words better suited to an occasion.

Madrigals are not intended to make a long evening. They share a family likeness. Neither is the beauty of flood lighting a joy forever. Its loveliness does not exactly increase. It was her understanding of such matters that made Mrs. Manifold such a successful producer. The program of music under the bridge was designed to last forty-five minutes and no longer. Tonight they were anxious minutes as the black clouds piled up behind Lacy woods. But still the rain held off, and at last the final notes of "The Silver Swan" faded along the water.

Mrs. Manifold let her stopwatch run for thirty seconds. Then, pressing an electric button, she gave a signal to the men

180

who waited a little distance beyond the lake. A minute later a company of rockets tore into the air, broke into gunfire and then fell slowly in chandeliers of stars, hovering over the water. And every person on the shore said "Oooh!" and every duck in the rushes said "Squawk!" and "Poor things!" said Amy Caske. "They must be dreadfully frightened. But it's only once a year."

A second company of rockets raced into the sky, and a third: and then, just as the stars died in the darkness, a natural firework stabbed the clouds, and thunder rolled above the hill. Spots of rain began to fall, and at once the crowd, shuffling into coats and raising umbrellas, hurried towards cars and motor coaches.

Mrs. Manifold hastened to the water's edge. "We made it," she said. "Well done, Anatole!"

"Thanks be," said Anatole Bysshe.

And Lady Gossamer, after her fashion, said, "Of course everyone will be *soaked*. It's *too* dreadful. I knew it would be like this, but you wouldn't listen. I do hope poor Lady Bexminster gets away in time."

"Do you want a lift?" Davie asked Miss Bangle, "or have you got your car?"

"Yes, I have, thank you."

"Then run like a rabbit. Don't wait for me."

"I won't."

"Goodnight. I enjoyed hearing and seeing it with you."

"So did I," said Miss Bangle, disappearing into the crowd as another flash of lightning illumined the lake and the thunder followed ominously nearer.

Some of the company went to the house to wait for their cars at the great door. Davie was one of these. He stood under the portico, watching the lightning, waiting for a car that was unexpectedly late.

And then a voice behind him said, "Excuse me—are you Dr. Davie?"

"Yes," said Davie, turning. "I am."

"My name's Rowan, and I'm a colleague of Philip Gossamer."

"I know you by sight."

"You do?"

"Yes—we sat next each other at lunch on Saturday."

"Of course we did. I've a message for you. You were expecting a car from the King William, I believe."

"Yes."

"They've had trouble and they're sorry but they can't make it. They said they'd try to get you a car from somewhere else—but that's doubtful, and I said they weren't to bother. I can fix you up."

"That's very good of you."

"Not a bit. I'll be very glad to drive you back myself."

"Are you sure that's not out of your way?"

"No. It's nothing."

"Thank you very much."

"If you're ready, let's go. The storm won't wait. I reckon we've got about ten minutes before the cataclysm. My car's round the corner. We can get away at once."

It was still only spotting with rain as Alec Rowan led Davie down the gravel sweep to the left.

"Where do you live, Mr. Rowan?"

"Bexminster."

"But look here—that's two sides of a triangle. It *is* out of your way."

"No, it's not. What's a mile or so one way or another? Hop in."

"I must say it seems an imposition."

They set off across the park, following a line of red taillights that raced and twisted ahead of them. And suddenly the rain came down in a sheet of water.

Halfway across the park the road divides. The track to the right leads towards the main gates, where the road through the lanes to Bexminster wheels to the right, and the road to King's Lacy runs straight ahead. All the cars were following this right-hand fork. But Alec Rowan turned to the left.

"I'm a little lost," said Davie presently. "I thought we ought to go down the other road for the main gates and King's Lacy."

"Not necessarily. That's the official way."

They drove on.

Davie loved driving at night. He liked to watch the hills and valleys in the surface of the road, caught in the car lights—the weird geography of an insect's world: he liked the trees racing towards him out of the shadows and disappearing as suddenly into the night: and he liked all the eyes that glitter in the dark. But there was no pleasure in this. There was nothing to see but the rain. There were not even any car lights bobbing about ahead of them.

"I'm sorry to sound a fusspot and an unbeliever," he said. "You ought to know. Indeed, you must know. But it seems to me that we're going the wrong way. Where are you taking me?"

"For a ride," said Mr. Rowan.

Davie said nothing to that. He could think of nothing appropriate to say. This was rural England, not prohibition Chicago. And surely the managing director of Bexminster Electronics was not insane.

They drove on. And then, at a place where the road dipped down into a hollow, the headlights picked out a grove of oak trees on the left. And waiting beside the oak trees in the glistening rain Davie perceived two cars. Alec Rowan passed them, turned off the road onto the turf, drew up, and switched off his engine.

What the devil, thought Davie, but still he said nothing.

Behind him in the darkness two car doors opened and shut. A few seconds later, the door of Rowan's car opened and two men pushed into the back seat.

"Well," said Rowan, "here we all are."

He switched off the headlights. Then he turned on the light in the roof. And instantly the windscreen was transformed into a witch's looking glass. There was no need to turn round. Against the black quicksilver of the night Dr. Davie found himself regarding the faces of Mr. Caske and Mr. Major. They were not friendly faces.

"What now, gentlemen?" he asked.

"I'll tell you, Dr. Davie," said Alec Rowan.

IV

"But this is absurd," said Davie, five minutes later. "You have been totally mistaken. You think—"

"I *know*," said Alec Rowan. "I know that you have been fiddling around, looking for information about Bexminster Electronics. I am the managing director of that firm and it's my business to protect it. Nobody's going to hurt you. But we have to have the truth. You will perhaps think this is all very melodramatic. If you do, then I must suggest to you that it's no more melodramatic than your creeping upstairs to Miss Jesmond's room and secretly going through her property. We want to know why. We want to know why you scraped an acquaintance with Joe Major: why you represented yourself to Miss Jesmond as being a friend of his: why you took such an interest in those doodles that Miss

Jesmond was collecting: and why—why most of all—you went back there."

Davie waited several seconds before replying. The others sat quietly watching him. Precisely in the silence the thunder of the dying storm rolled in the distance. It was (Davie thought) all rather like an early Dickens novel, with the weather nicely appropriate to the plot. Then, "I'm sorry, gentlemen," he said. "I do realize that my behaviour must have seemed very strange to you, and that it's very reasonable that you should suppose that I have been snooping on your private affairs. I assure you I haven't. I have been concerned to find out who murdered Jiří Vanásek—and that means, also, who murdered your secretary, Robert Coppleston."

"Are you connected with the police?" asked Daniel Caske.

"That's the trouble. I am not. I am just someone who wants to know the answer."

"And have you found it?"

"I think so."

"You have?" said Alec Rowan. "Then perhaps you'll be good enough to tell us. We need to know the answer too. If you can tell us, you may perhaps explain your behaviour at the same time."

"I think I shall."

"Well, then—tell us."

"It was Coppleston's death that came first to my notice— and as I had been in the hall at the King William towards the end of his telephone call, I was, from the beginning, aware of two things. One, that his call resulted from some unexpected emergency, and two, that the emergency was so recent, and so evidently secret, that nobody else could have been informed on the matter, unless he had overheard the call, or some part of it. Now the lounge door was going through its long act of closing—which meant that someone had just gone into the room—and so it seemed to me that somebody could have overheard the call, but, naturally, I hadn't the smallest idea who he might be. There were many people in the lounge. The only ones I was aware of were Mr. Rowan, Mr. Caske, and Mr. Major."

As he named them Davie turned in his seat and looked at the two men behind him. And they stared back at him. Nobody spoke.

"I put that aside in my mind," said Davie, turning back and addressing the faces in the windscreen. "I couldn't take the problem any further without better evidence."

"So I should hope," said Daniel Caske.

"It was the death of Jiří Vanásek which concerned me more nearly, and which offered more opportunities for investigation—and it seemed obvious that the two crimes were connected. One man was killed because he had found and unfortunately had understood a message. The other was killed because he had lost his reputation as a letter-box, and because he was heard talking—to me—about giving the business up and going to the police.

"The first thing that caught my attention in the Vanásek case was the question of time. To begin with I thought Mr. Major had made a mistake when he said that he had been visited by Mr. Carroll at twenty-five minutes past eleven. But when he told me that he hadn't put his clock back that night before going to bed, I realized (provided he was telling the truth) that someone else must have done it for him—and that that somebody needn't have put it back a mere five or ten minutes. He could have put it back half an hour or forty minutes: in which case someone arriving at the house at eleven twenty-five might really have been arriving at five past twelve. Mr. Major was entirely vague about time: he would have been none the wiser."

"Too true," murmured Joe Major behind him.

"Now if the clock *had* been put back it would make a perfect sworn alibi for someone. Half an hour to commit a murder—and yet to be able to go from A to B in the proper time. Say Mr. Carroll from the Bear to Brook Lane in two minutes. Or," Davie went on after a short pause, "Sir Philip from the Bear to Lacy in not much longer.

"And then I had another thought: there could have been two people concerned: one to put the clock back and one to take advantage of it. I had no evidence of that. I just pigeonholed it in my mind."

"I don't see why you should indulge in such remote calculations," said Alec Rowan. "What was Joe Major's clock to you?"

"Nothing, if it hadn't recorded that Mr. Carroll walked down the alley at twenty-five past eleven. No one walked down the alley at that time—unless it were on tiptoe. But someone did walk down it at about two minutes past twelve. He was seen by Miss Muffin—the girl who calls herself Madame Jeanne."

"All right. Go on."

"My next speculation was about the doodles—Miss Jesmond's entertaining collection of doodles made by directors during meetings."

"My God!" said Daniel Caske.

"The note in Vanásek's shop had been torn off something. It contained two dates. When I saw those same dates on three of those papers, it occurred to me that the note might have been torn off Mr. Carroll's paper. One couldn't tell, because Mr. Carroll was in the habit of making boats out of his memorandum papers."

"He was," said Joe Major.

"The boat that he made on this occasion was smaller than usual—which suggested a smaller paper. And I found out—I'm afraid Mr. Rowan knows how I found out—that something *had* been torn off Mr. Carroll's paper.

"At first I thought someone else might have unfolded the boat, cut off the paper, and remade the boat. But then I realized that in that case there would have been two sets of creases. There weren't. That meant Carroll must have cut the paper himself before making the boat. Well . . . perhaps he wanted to keep that bit of news; or perhaps he didn't—perhaps he left it on the table or dropped it. At any rate somebody used it, and somebody had to find it."

Alec Rowan stirred in his seat. "All these things are hunches, guesses. Who found the paper? Who tore the bit off? Who made use of it? Who put the clock back? You pose all these questions. You don't answer them.

"I will. The answer to all of them came to me this morning in Mrs. Bazeley's shop. On Monday morning early Mrs. Bazeley—who is a very remarkable woman, immeasurably greedy, entirely ruthless where her interests are concerned—on Monday early Mrs. Bazeley called at George's, walked into the office and removed a piece of china which she coveted beyond the limits of her endurance. She wrapped it in a silk handkerchief, which she thought was Jiří Vanásek's. It wasn't. And I had seen that handkerchief before. Or, at least, I was pretty sure I had."

"That sounds better," said Daniel Caske.

"And yes, I thought, that fixes the Vanásek case—but what about Coppleston? If the same man committed both crimes—and then I suddenly understood. I had been wasting my time wondering who had opened that lounge door. It didn't matter a damn who had walked through the hall.

188

Coppleston's telephone call wasn't *over*heard by anyone. It was just *heard*. Heard by Mr. Carroll."

For ten seconds there was total silence in the car.

"You mean . . ." began Joe Major, and stopped.

"Yes; I do. I think the man who was betraying your secrets was William Carroll."

"But only on Saturday," said Joe Major, "he was talking to me most seriously about leaks in our organization and how—"

"I think he is a great actor, Mr. Major—playing a part, and enjoying playing a part, as the person most anxious to solve mysteries of his own creation. It is a familiar trick of the confidence man. Coppleston wasn't the chap to keep quiet about anything affecting the interests of his company. If he had suspicions he would have to be silenced. I think Carroll met him in the drive, took him on an alleged short cut through the rhododendrons and killed him. Killed him with a blow at a vital spot—a commando blow—and Coppleston's hands would have been occupied with his bicycle."

"William was a commando," said Joe Major.

"So I guessed. What he meant to do about getting rid of the body we may never know—but he had a tremendous piece of luck when old Dew saw the handlebars shining in the darkness. If there had been any footprints among the bushes they were made sense of now by the pair of them tramping in. And there was Dew to witness Carroll's surprise and concern. It was far better for Carroll that he should be present himself when the discovery was made.

"Except for one thing—except for one thing. Nowadays crimes are solved by hairs, by threads, by fibers. The police have found fibers caught on the bushes. Some belong to Coppleston's coat, one perhaps to Carroll's blue suit, none to Mr. Dew's clothes—he was wearing a mackintosh. But there are several others. William Carroll wasn't wearing his blue suit in the afternoon. He should have thought of that. He was wearing his gardening clothes. That's what they'll get him on, gentlemen—not on my hunches and guesses. Don't think I don't venerate the police."

"And Vanásek?"

"I don't think Carroll knew what to do about Vanásek until, coming down the alley, he heard him telling me about his blackmail, and discussing the possibility of going to the police. When he realized we were going out through the shop, and that the back door was still open, I think he suddenly saw his chance and decided on the spur of the moment to take Vanásek by surprise. There was some small struggle in which he lost his handkerchief—but didn't notice it. Then he left by the front door. I think he did that because he didn't want to be seen creeping out of the back gate. And he did want to come down the full length of the alley as though he had just come from the Bear. Then he called on Mr. Major, and, while he was there, I think he put the clock back."

"I went into the kitchen to get him a glass."

"Exactly—and I expect he knew more about clocks than you do, Mr. Major. It wouldn't have done if you'd realized next day that the clock was half an hour slow: but he knew that you never would. *He* knew that the clock would stop at about four minutes to twelve—after he'd left—and that you would think it had stopped 'of its own sweet obstinate will.'

"He had a bit of luck, too, with the lost ring. That was intended to consolidate the alibi. It would have sounded well enough if he had had to telephone to you about it—but it would have been no proof of where he actually was. But your telephoning to him was indeed proof that he had gone straight home after leaving you. He ought to have had a pretty good alibi from the time he left Lacy to the time he got home to Combe Magna. And he *would* have had one, seeing that a clock can't go into the witness box—except for fingerprints which of course he didn't leave—if he hadn't lost his handkerchief.

"The extraordinary thing about this man is his boldness. He didn't attempt to keep out of the way, he went to the Festival entertainments without turning a hair. You'd have thought he'd have avoided Vanásek's shop—but not at all. I think he may have been the man who called there early on Monday morning. Perhaps it was only then that he realized that he'd lost his handkerchief, and if he did know that the back door was not bolted, he may have hoped to find it. Unfortunately for him, Mrs. Bazeley had got there first. But I won't bother you with Mrs. Bazeley. That's something different."

Davie glanced at Alec Rowan.

"Too much guesswork? I know. But in case you're thinking this is all a colossal yarn, I must point out that William Carroll was not at the party tonight. He was—how shall I put it?—unavoidably detained."

"I see," said Alec Rowan. "And I've made an enormous mistake. You mustn't blame the King William. I have to admit that I rang them up and told them not to come. I hope I haven't scared you too much."

"I was a little frightened, I admit, for a few minutes," said Davie serenely. "But not really. Not really. You see I'd spent two hours at the police station this morning. I knew it wasn't you who had killed Vanásek and Coppleston. So I didn't think you were likely to kill *me*."

"I'm sorry to have taken such a liberty—"

"With my liberty. It's all right. I quite understand."

191

"Dr. Davie," said Joe Major. "I wonder if I might offer you a lift back to King's Lacy."

Davie laughed delightedly.

"If you're quite sure," he said, "that that won't take you out of your way, I shall be most grateful."

V

Lying awake in Judge Jeffreys's bedroom, Davie was thinking about guesses and hunches and proofs. The Judge would not have been scrupulous in this matter. Modern justice was more demanding. Mr. Coombes could show that the clock had been put back, but there was no proof at all how much it had been put back or by whom.

Certainly there were difficulties: but surely his deductions had indicated the right person. Knowing where to look, the police would find what they needed. Already they had the fibers caught in the bushes. Already they had the handwriting on the bit of paper. There might be fingerprints on the doors. There was the handkerchief, light blue with the dark blue edge.

And there was the boat, he was thinking as he snuggled himself into precisely the right position. He was glad he had behaved so badly about that.

Two minutes later, as he crossed the borders of sleep, Dr. Davie was smiling. He had just remembered George Canackers and Mildred Meade-Fuller.